9TH STORY PUBLISHING

# THELIFT

## NINE STORIES OF TRANSFORMATION

### VOLUME ONE

Edited by Daniel Foytik
and Scarlett R. Algee

Cover art & interior illustrations: Jeannette Andromeda

Logo design and formatting: Greg Shaffer

ISBN: 978-0-578-40881-1

Please visit us online at victoriaslift.com to learn more about The Lift and hear the audio drama featuring many more stories of Victoria and her very special Lift.

9th Story Studios | PO Box 97925 | Pittsburgh, PA 15227

*Praise for The Lift, Nine Stories of Transformation:*

*"Fans of the **The Lift** podcast will love the stories of ruin and redemption in this powerhouse anthology, and newcomers will quickly discover that riding with the creepy childlike elevator-operator, Victoria, isn't a journey easily forgotten. Nine tales of transformative terror and valor from some of the most diabolically beautiful writers working today."*

> *~Jessica McHugh, author of **Rabbits in the Garden** and **Nightly Owl, Fatal Raven***

*"Victoria Bigglesworth-Hayes is a perplexing character as she presents initially as a creepy child, but her ultimate purpose seems to be restoration for those who have taken a wrong turn in life. This anthology features nine stories that take the reader deeper into the world of Victoria and **The Lift**, which has its origins as a podcast. These stories range from chillingly endearing to terrifying, and **all** are entertaining. Climb aboard **The Lift** for an unforgettable ride.*

> *~Diane Student, creator and host of the **History Goes Bump Podcast***

*"A wicked variety of woven magic that introduces familiar or new people to the legend of Victoria. Through the ages, this collection is one hell of a ride!"*

> *~Paul Sating, creator of the **Who Killed Julie Audio Drama***

*Reviews of The Lift, Audio Drama Podcast:*

*The Lift* has an average 4.9 stars (out of 5) rating on Apple Podcasts. Here's what some of the listeners have said:

*I found this podcast on accident, and oh what a happy accident it was. I ended up binging the entire season in 2 days. The different writers bringing their own perspective of the same story, added with an amazing production value makes this an easy addictive favorite. Even my kids love to listen, we try to guess before each episode how it will go; will Victoria be a sweet benevolent spirit.... righting the wrongs of the world, or will a vicious wraith of vengeance??? Please keep us guessing, the dichotomy is what keeps this show fresh and amazing!!! Thanks for the entertainment!!!* **Arkenz2011**

*If I had to pick one podcast I couldn't live without...it will always be The Lift. The stories pull me into Victoria's world and I find myself feeling a range of emotions for the poor souls who find themselves making a choice. The show is a representation of our own lives and the choices we struggle to make each day. Much respect and thanks to all of the creators responsible for putting this podcast together, you've made every episode one of the highlights of each week.* **Ryanmkd**

*What do you get when you mix; Dante's Inferno with Dickens - A Christmas Carol with a heavy dash of the Twilight Zone. You get this great new creation of THE LIFT. A episodic tale with a charming English ghost acting as our Virgil, Rod Sterling, and ghost or past present and future. It is charming, and spooky, and uplifting and illuminating!* **Eric from Buffalo**

*This podcast is amazing. It takes paranormal into the reality of decisions and possible paths we all face throughout our lives. This may sound weird, but in a way, listening to all of the character's dilemmas and see them decide how to face what they fear has helped me face my own locked up truths. Thank you for making this podcast. I truly love it. Victoria is brilliant. Please keep doing what you do. . .* **CarlaKovitz**

# Dedication

For all of those who have found in Victoria and *The Lift* redemption, solace, or simply the special nourishment of the soul that comes from a story shared, this collection is for you.

And, for those coming to ride The Lift for the first time, we, the storytellers who have been invited to share Victoria's world and wisdom with you, hope you find the same happiness many others before you have found in this strange, lost place and, for a little while, it may lift you up as well.

# Table of Contents

EXTRAS:

MUSIC FROM THE LIFT AUDIODRAMA
Henninger Parke Music / We Talk of Dreams

DRAWINGS FROM THE JOURNALS OF
W.E. BIGGLESWORTH-HAYES
by Daniel Foytik & Jeanette Andromeda

THE COLLECTED NOTES OF ALICE MARGARET
BIGGLESWORTH-HAYES
by Cynthia Lowman

ABOUT OUR AUTHORS AND ILLUSTRATOR

THANK YOU

# FOREWORD
## by Owl Goingback

**M**ake a decision. Choose. Sounds simple, doesn't it? And for the most part, it usually is: salt or pepper, mustard or catchup, one lump or two, shorts or long pants, drive to work or take the bus. Some decisions are a little more complex, casting larger ripples on otherwise calm waters: sleep in or go to work, stay out drinking or go home and go to bed, do what the boss says or tell him to shove it, go through with the marriage or hop the next bus out of town.

But what if the decision we had to make would change everything about our existence, granting us possible redemption for our mistakes, changing a life and death moment in time, or condemning us to an eternity of searching for a way out of the darkness? Could you make such a choice? Do you have the courage to open a door to the unknown and face your biggest fears?

What if the life changing choice you had to make was being offered to you by a ghostly little girl in blonde pigtails, and a vintage dress, who carried a music box that emitted a haunting melody and an eerie green glow? What then? Would you even believe what your eyes were seeing? Or would you think it all just a bad dream, a nightmare, caused by too much work, far too much stress, or simply brought on by that piece of aged beef you had for dinner?

But the little girl with the quaint English accent is as real as everything else in The Lost Place, a world of shadows and dangers that exists within the dusty hallways of a nine-story Victorian building. A dilapidated structure that can only be seen, and entered, by those who have been invited. Her name is Victoria, and she operates the antique lift of wood and tarnished brass. But she is much more than a mere elevator operator, and far more than meets the eyes. She is also a guide, leading all those who have been invited to their ultimate destiny.

The invited have a decision to make, and it just may be the most important decision of their lives. They will have to choose whether or not to enter the lift, waiting with sweaty palms and bated breath, as Victoria presses the button that will send the elevator creaking and rattling to one of the floors above. And then they will have to decide if they have the courage to face what waits for them behind one of wooden doors lining the dark and empty hallways. Some will find forgiveness and salvation, mercy for their sins, and a chance to start life anew. Others will find–

Well, let's not spoil the surprise. Instead, come along for the ride. There's plenty of room on the lift, and I'm sure Victoria won't mind one more passenger. She might even let you listen to her music box.

Through the storytelling of nine extremely gifted writers, you will experience the jealousy of rival siblings, the seduction of greed and power, the longing of a woman who would do anything to be a mother, and the callousness of a Las Vegas con artist. You will know fear as you witness an apocalyptic world through the eyes of someone considered far less than human, feel the white-knuckled rush of adrenalin as you go on a suicide mission against the Imperial Japanese Navy, and know what it is like to face your biggest fear and doubt.

So, step aboard the lift, and see what Victoria has in store for you. Maybe in the end, the little girl with the blonde pigtails will also ask you to make a choice.

Choose wisely.

Owl Goingback
Bram Stoker Award-winning author of **Crota**
2018

Hello. My name is Victoria, and I've been waiting for <u>you</u>.

*Are you lost? I was lost.*

Darkness has gathered around us. These are times of fear, doubt, and anger, but they lead to a path you must not travel.

*I will be your light. I will save you - <u>IF</u> you let me.*

Your future will unfold based on the choices you make here and now. Choose wisely.

*Can you see the path? I will try to guide you.*

Face your fears and move beyond them. They are chains that hold you and bind you to your past.

*You already hold the key to unshackle yourself.*

Come along now, let's go for a ride.

The Basement: Things Best Locked Away

# Brothers' Keeper
## by Brooke Warra

The two men sat for a long time without speaking. Each had known the other for so long that each was sure he knew what the other was thinking. Between them sat an untouched plate of duck and three empty bottles of wine. One man drank for pleasure, the other to calm the shaking of his hands. Each man wore a top hat and tuxedo, one in fine cloth, the other in tattered crushed velvet and patches at the elbows. Both men were the cause of many stares from the many other patrons in the upscale downtown restaurant, where the city's finest dined. The man in the worn red velvet jacket pulled at the curled ends of his handlebar mustache. The other tucked a boutonniere back into his breast pocket and poured himself another glass of wine.

"None for me, Octavio," the other said.

"Come now, Alistair," Octavio said. "We are businessmen, let us have a glass of wine together."

Both men spoke in an affected European accent that sounded as if it could have originated anywhere between the isles near northern Scotland to the confessional booths of Italy to the whorehouses of

Amsterdam, depending on how deep they were in their cups. Both men had been born and raised in the Midwestern United States.

"You've had plenty for the both of us," Alistair said, gesturing to the bottles that littered the table. A spilled drop of wine bloomed like a bruise across the white cloth. The duck sat, greasy and attracting flies. Alistair thought for a moment that it was always this way with Octavio. Like a scavenger circling carrion.

He felt the eyes of the other patrons burning into the back of his head.

*And with an audience,* he thought.

"If you're worried about the price…" Octavio patronized.

"Hmph." Alistair waved a hand. "It's always money with you."

"Oh, does the money not matter to you, brother?"

Alistair refused to give Octavio a reply. Instead he rolled a cigarette between his yellowed fingertips, the candlelight reflecting off the many rubies of his many rings. A show. The stones were as fake as the accent.

"Shall we get down to it, then?" his brother asked. He sounded German.

"I will not sell them!" Alistair slammed his fist onto the table, rocking the duck from its plate and igniting a swarm of flies.

Octavio smiled, plucked the rolled cigarette from his brother's fist, and lit it. He clapped his hands. "Bravo. You were always good with the theatrics,

3

brother," he said. "Probably why you were always better in the tents. Those people in the risers need to hear you." He thumped his own chest. "You must project from the lungs! Me, myself, I've always been better behind the scenes. Running the show, unseen. No podium for me."

Octavio chuckled. Alistair glared.

"No, of course, Octavio, you've never wanted the attention," Alistair said, spitting the last word.

They both knew who was lying.

"Why should you keep them, Alistair? What could they possibly mean for you except a bunch of misshapen, mealy mouths to feed? Are you even traveling by train anymore? Last I heard, you were all touring in a caravan of automobiles with the bumpers glued on. It would be funny, like a circus clown-car, if it weren't so pathetic, Alistair. Eh?"

Alistair straightened his spine, sitting up taller than his brother, who swayed drunkenly in his own seat.

"They're like my own family. Like my own children. You don't *sell* your family."

Octavio threw his head back and laughed, an uproarious, ostentatious laugh that grated on Alistair's nerves. The hair on his arms stood on end.

"Can you *buy* family, though? I wonder," Octavio said when he caught his breath.

Alistair clenched his hands, opening and closing his fists. The thought of punching Octavio square in the face crossed his mind. Instead, he reached for the half-empty bottle of wine and said, "I think I'll take that drink now after all. Order us a bottle of rum, though, brother. What are we, conformists?"

He poured himself a drink, then tore a wing from the putrefying duck and stuck it in his mouth.

He had found them one by one. Rescued them, really. Some from their own families. Others from men in business suits, who would sell a stroke or a pinch to anyone off the street with a bit of coin. Some had found *him* and begged him to take them with him. The twins had been left on his office doorstep one cold November morning. That had been the beginning. Two squalling pink faces, in a bundle of blankets hiding their one-ness. Joined at the rib and hip, they'd come to be his first attraction, though not at first. At first he'd tried to find a home for them. After visiting many dirty, dark asylum corridors, and speaking with many a mad doctor and every swindler with dollar signs in his eyes, Alistair (who had then just been known as Joseph Baker, Attorney at Law), had had an idea. If this squirming ball of limbs and other-ness was destined to end up in an asylum or sideshow, peddled to every Tom-Dick-and-Harry with a fetish, why shouldn't he make a bit of money, and take care of them too? Why, he'd grown fond of them, perhaps even loved them, strange as they were to him and the world at large. Surely he could provide for them, and why shouldn't he profit from it?

That year had been 1922. A wondrous and lucrative year for Alistair and the twins, with many to follow. Along the way, they'd collected many orphans. The Fairy Girl, whose father kept her in a glass cage he'd had specially built inside her room, displaying her like a Fabergé egg to paying customers. The tiny, delicate, bird-like little girl had delighted in the train rides between cities, and being carried around in the crook of the arms of the other freaks, mostly by Velma, the Wolf-Man (they dressed her in men's clothes for performances), who was her favorite. Then had come their own Lobster Twins; a Medium, who was just a 12-year-old runaway Alistair had taken pity on and taught to read the Tarot; and finally the Human Torso.

They had all become a family. They took care of each other. Rejoiced in their successes and shared each other's failures. Velma and The Torso had even married and had a child together. When the child failed to thrive and passed away, it was a blow to the entire troupe. They had taken several weeks off, holed up in a seashore hotel together, and recovered.

Together.

Alistair spared no expense. They traveled in the finest conditions, on the best railways, ate the most exquisite fare, wore the choicest linens. His freaks were royalty.

For a time.

The public that had kept them in luxury one nickel at a time had become disinterested, had stopped attending. There were protests. It wasn't becoming to gawk and stare at the deformed and less fortunate any longer. The novelty wore off. Human interest groups had had a field day. It was after the war. Things were different now.

Their finances dwindled. No more were the accommodations of the highest caliber. They'd been forced to purchase several run-down sedans from a used-car lot in Omaha last winter. Alistair hated to admit it, but Octavio's jest about the bumpers being held fast with glue wasn't entirely untrue. They'd sold and pawned most of their luxury items to pay for the vehicles. The Fairy Girl had the hardest time of it, clinging with tear-filled eyes to her leather-bound, gilt-paged *Complete Works of Shakespeare*. Finally, she had parted with it and they had all piled into their rusty, noisy caravan and completed their tour.

They'd panhandled and bartered and begged their way across the landscape. Performed at drive-ins where the intoxicated audience, who'd expected a peep show, threw concession food and beer bottles at them. One had struck Velma in the face, and she had refused to perform at the next venue. How could Alistair blame her? There were many more such events at local bars, carnivals, roadside stops, even a child's birthday party in Denver that had gone horribly awry.

By the time Octavio telegraphed him about a meeting in New York City, Alistair was desperate. He had hoped that his estranged brother, with his connections and success on the vaudeville stage, could provide temporary lodgings, perhaps some capital… Just to get them through the tough times. This passing fad of activism against the freak show would subside. The public was fickle. They'd be back.

Instead, Octavio had offered to buy his freaks – his family! – from him. Imagine! Trading living breathing humans for a fistful of paper. The thought of Octavio managing his people sickened Alistair. Octavio and his slickery, his twisted smile, his ego, his… His fetishes!

"Vaudeville is the last stop for them, Alistair," Octavio had said when Alistair had rung him at his nightclub shortly after receiving the message. "I would be taking a hit for you. I would be doing you a favor."

Alistair had placed the phone back into its cradle, tipped the host at the hotel where they were staying that night, and watched his freaks through the window for a while. They were in the courtyard playing a game of hopscotch. Other hotel guests watched them with alternating looks of fascination and disgust. Some threw coins at their feet. His people played, clapping their hands, throwing back their heads to reveal mouths full of misshapen, lumpy teeth, releasing gales of unadulterated laughter.

They were unaware. Only The Torso had an inkling of their dire situation. Alistair often consulted with Manny about the books, the tours, the clients. Manny, if he'd been born into any other body, would have made a fine businessman in another life. Wasn't he one in this life? If Alistair hadn't let the money intoxicate him in those first few years, if he'd just heeded Manny's warnings about the future, perhaps they wouldn't be in this mess.

But they were. And now, what to do about Octavio?

Alistair held his brother up as Octavio vomited into a trash bin on the street outside the bar they'd just been thrown out of. Earlier, they'd been tossed from the restaurant when Octavio had begun making lewd suggestions to the female patrons at the neighboring tables.

"Did you see her?" Octavio asked. He stood suddenly, nearly falling into the puddle of his own sick, and wiped the sleeve of his expensive jacket across his mouth. "Just there – now! – did you see her?"

"Oh, not this again," Alistair said. "After all these years, are you still on about the little girl with green eyes and – ?"

"And the music box," Octavio finished. "Yes. Didn't you see her?"

Octavio stared down the empty street, his face drained of color. Alistair sighed.

Ever since their boyhood, Octavio had claimed to be haunted by a little girl and her mysterious music box. Their parents, God-fearing farm people, stared at each other across the breakfast table whenever Octavio, then Paul, had regaled the family with tall tales of the little girl's visits.

9

"She never looks at me," he'd said, staring dreamily at his stack of pancakes one morning. "It's like she doesn't know I'm even there... But then, why does she come?"

He would spend hours at the family piano, attempting to recreate the haunting, melancholy tune he'd heard her music box play, to no avail. "I can't remember!" he'd yell, and slam his fists against the keys, which usually drew a sharp rebuke from their mother.

Alistair had heard their parents discussing the possibility of taking his brother in to "see someone" on many occasions. Mortified, their father had said it was simply a matter of "getting the boy's head out of the clouds". The decision had been made that Octavio would quit his art and music lessons and join their father on the farm in the mornings for work. Alistair, on the other hand, suffered no hallucinations about ghostly little girls and trinket boxes, and so was allowed to continue his lessons. Octavio would never forgive him for it.

Alistair's older brother had been bright and talented. Music, poetry, even dance had come naturally to the boy at a young age. This had been much to the delight of their mother, and much to the dismay of their father.

"He's got promise," their mother had said, echoing the words of Octavio's instructors. There had been arguing late into the night, but ultimately both boys had been enrolled in lessons. A woman came three times a week to teach them music and piano.

Saturdays, an art teacher. Until the visions had started. After that, Octavio rose every day at four and didn't return until late into the evening, filthy, sore, and exhausted. Alistair, who'd been permitted to stay behind but was expected to take his music doubly seriously, played piano late into the night while his brother slept off his exhaustion.

Truth be told, Alistair had been relieved to be rid of Octavio. Talented and artistic, his older brother had also been cruel, often punishing him, it seemed, just for existing. Not a day went by that Octavio wasn't waiting for him around a corner, ready to pounce. He'd seemed to take joy in his brother's weariness of him. Alistair would carry a scar above his right eye well into adulthood after Octavio had seen fit to push him from their second-story bedroom window after a dispute over a toy train. He hadn't fallen, much to Octavio's disappointment, but he had broken through the glass pane and cut himself. Their mother had burst through the door, alerted by the sound of shattering glass, before Octavio could make use of the shards in his state of anger. Even with all those hours spent in the fields working, he had still found time to inflict his violence on Alistair. His fetish for brutality had extended beyond his younger brother, and was often focused on ant hills or the neighbor's pets.

Just before the lessons had been revoked, their mother had caught him again, this time with a stray cat in the barn. He'd just finished tying a knot in the rope around its neck and seemed to be contemplating what to do next when she'd happened to come looking for

11

their father, and instead found her oldest child in the barn just before a diabolical act.

Heartbroken and shaken, she'd asked Octavio, "Does *she* tell you to do these things, son?"

It had been an especially eventful day. Earlier, he had shut Alistair's hands in the fallboard of the piano. The younger boy would wear bandages for weeks, forgoing his lessons while he healed. Octavio had insisted it was an accident, and their mother, at her wit's end with the boy, had sent him outside "until your father comes home" while she thought of what she should do with him. It had only been a short while before she went in search of him, when she'd found Octavio with the cat. The terrified creature had clawed her hands to shreds as she loosened the rope around its neck, and shot off like a bolt of lightning into the shadows of the barn, howling.

She sat on the firewood chopping block and put her hands over her face. "Be truthful with me, son. Does *she* put these ideas in your head?"

Just that morning, another visit by the specter child had been told over eggs and toast.

"No!" Octavio had yelled in frustration. "I *told* you! She doesn't even *look at me*. Nobody looks at me."

Later, when their father returned home from his work in the fields and was made aware of the events of the day, he'd finally had enough. Their mother had protested, but he'd said something about "idle hands" and "the devil's work," and the decision was final. Octavio would join him at dawn every morning, and

Alistair would be allowed to continue his education, pending any talk of spectral visions.

After hearing the verdict handed down by their father, Alistair returned to the bedroom he shared with Octavio and relayed the information. Octavio had said nothing, but the room became deathly silent as he contemplated a childhood spent working the fields.

Mostly as a way to break the silence, Alistair had asked his brother, "Is it true?"

"Is what true?"

"Do you really see her every night? What does she do?"

Octavio had rolled toward the wall then and said, "Nothing. She stares at you."

The violence hadn't entirely ceased afterward, but it had slowed. Octavio never forgave Alistair his education, and made sure to remind him of it often. The two had parted ways as soon as they were old enough to leave the farm, Alistair with a scholarship for law school and Octavio with a knapsack and dreams of the city lights of New York. Until the twins had shown up outside his office, Alistair had had no desire to continue pursuing show business. All those hours spent at the piano, reciting poetry, and learning to sing from his diaphragm had been for naught, it seemed. But the twins had changed it all. The money they'd made him allowed for a top-rate production. He'd been surprised at how much he enjoyed it: the long hours on the road, the hundreds of eager faces in the crowd, the short-lived affair with a trapeze artist or two. Occasionally he'd come across a review of Octavio's productions, but the two hadn't spoken since their childhood. The older man seemed to be making a name for himself on the stage just as Alistair was gaining celebrity on the traveling circuit. When the press caught wind that the two were brothers, there were many telegrams and phone calls requesting a joint interview. Both denied these inquiries. The mysterious feud between them caused much speculation in the back pages of gossip rags.

Their mother, on her deathbed, had conceded to an interview with one of these papers, and made it her dying wish that the two of them reconcile and "behave like family." Neither of them could scarcely afford to continue avoiding each other after that. They risked alienating an adoring public by disregarding the final wishes of their own mother. They had compromised, and made a deal to meet once a year for these dinners. Neither enjoyed them. Octavio hadn't mentioned the ghost-child and her music box during these visits over the years, until now.

They stood in the street, listening for the sound of a music box. Alistair felt foolish.

"I can still hear the music." Octavio grabbed the sides of his head and shook it. "I –"

Without another word, he broke into a run.

"Hey!" Alistair ran after his brother, who disappeared around a corner and into an unlit alleyway. But there, the chase ended. Octavio was nowhere to be seen in the darkness of the alley.

"Come now, brother! It's late!" Alistair shouted, but was met with absolute silence. There wasn't even the sound of scurrying rats or alley cats. The noise from the street, club-goers stumbling drunkenly arm-in-arm, bands playing the last song of the night, seemed to be far, far away, even though it was only feet away.

Alistair felt the hair on his arms and neck rise. He took a step toward the street behind him. Not willing to turn his back on the darkness, he backed out, keeping his eyes fixed on the spot where his brother had disappeared. "I'm going home now! I've had enough of this, Octavio!"

There was no reply.

Back out on the street, in safety of the street lights, the din of the city's nightlife rushed to greet him. Alistair allowed himself now to be angry. It was just like his brother to pull some stunt like this.

"Well, he won't be getting what he came for," Alistair said aloud, thinking now of Octavio's persistent badgering about taking his troupe to New York. "No," he said, "he won't be getting them."

Determined now to make sure of it, Alistair stepped off the curb and hailed a nearby cab.

"Where to?" the driver asked once he was settled in the backseat.

"Fairview Campgrounds, just outside the city limits," he said.

The driver nodded. "That'll be extra."

"That's fine," Alistair said. Then, after a moment, "Say, you wouldn't happen to know of any filling stations open this time of night, would you?"

The first thing Alistair was aware of when he woke was that it was cold, a coldness he had never experienced before in all his life. A cold he could feel in his bones. Opening his eyes, he was met with absolute darkness. He could feel the ground beneath him, but could see and hear nothing. He was reminded of the alleyway he'd chased Octavio down the night before. Was that the night before? He couldn't recall. He wondered if he was dead.

"You are alive, Alistair," a voice said from the complete darkness that surrounded him.

Alistair jumped to his feet. "Where am I?"

A small light appeared then. It cast an unearthly green, and in its glow was the cherubic face of a young child. A little girl. A little girl, Alistair noted, holding a music box. The box seemed to be the source of the light.

"You!" Alistair took a step backward and was immediately met with a brick wall. He turned, pressing his hands against its cold, unforgiving surface. There was no door, at least not here. He shook his head. This was all too much to take in. Octavio had disappeared. Alistair couldn't remember anything else from the night before. He wasn't even sure how long he'd been out. And now he was here in this strange place with this girl – the ghost his brother had claimed to see every night of their shared childhood.

He slapped his own face, attempting to bring himself to his senses. "Get it together, Alistair!"

The little girl tilted her head to one side and looked puzzled. "You're not dreaming. This place is quite real. I'm real."

With those words, the room seemed to brighten a little. Alistair could make out a basement of sorts. Above, he heard the creaking of an elevator traveling through a shaft.

There's a way out, he thought.

"No. There is no way out," the little girl said, reading his thoughts.

The blood in Alistair's veins turned to ice.

"Well, save for one," she said, and took a step toward him.

"No! Don't come near me!" Alistair cried. He didn't like the look of that thick green light spilling from the music box like mist. It swirled around the girl's face, arms, and feet. At the sound of his shouting it seemed to grow, puff out, and reach for him. It smelled of a smoldering fire and though he had no way of being sure, he knew that if it touched him, it would burn. Alistair choked back a scream. He was too panicked to feel foolish over his fear of a small child.

"There *is* one way out," she said again, but made no move toward him. "If you choose wisely."

Alistair ran his hands through his hair and pulled, closing his eyes against the pain. "Wake up! Wake up!"

"You're not dreaming," the girl repeated. "Now, if you'll kindly stop this silliness and pay attention."

Upon opening his eyes, Alistair braved a second look at the girl. She looked like any other child; perhaps a bit pale. Her hair hung in blond ringlets at the sides of her face. She wore a dress with ruffled sleeves and a pair of Mary Jane dress shoes. She held the music box in her hands. It was dark, no longer spewing supernatural light.

She's just an ordinary girl, and *that* is just an ordinary music box, he told himself. Working to steady his heart rate, Alistair took several slow, deep breaths. He told himself it had been his panic that had caused him to see the ethereal mist reaching out for him. Just the shock of waking up in a strange place. The smell of fire was becoming overpowering. He looked around himself. The basement, if that's what this place was, seemed vast. The brick walls disappeared into what seemed like an eternal darkness. The room was huge and empty, save for himself and the child. If there was a fire, it must have been coming from another room.

"Do you smell smoke?" Alistair pressed his hands to the wall again, this time feeling for the heat of fire. The wall remained ice-cold.

"Do you?" the little girl asked. She didn't seem to be concerned that they were trapped inside a burning building.

"What's your name?" he asked her once his breathing had slowed.

"Victoria," she said.

"Well, Victoria, I don't know about you, but I'm getting out of here," he said, and turned on his heel and ran. He wasn't going to stay here and burn to death. He would get to safety and figure out where Octavio had gone afterward. Better yet, to hell with Octavio. He'd just get to safety and never think of his brother or Victoria ever again. He placed a hand against the bricks as he ran, feeling for a door. The darkness was so complete he couldn't see what lay before him. After only a few steps, he wasn't able to discern anything in the blackness behind him, either. The pale light around Victoria grew smaller and smaller, until it winked out entirely and the darkness swallowed her up.

"Don't you want to know where your brother is, Alistair? He's here too. He had his own crimes to answer for."

Alistair blinked. He was standing again in the circle of light, the brick wall to his back, and Victoria in front of him.

"How –?" Alistair spun around, again placing his hand against the wall, and again running full force into the dark. Again, he found himself standing in front of Victoria in the blink of an eye. The effect was dizzying. "What's happening to me?"

"There's no use trying that," she said matter-of-factly. "It will just bring you back every time."

She made no mention of what "it" was, and Alistair dared not ask.

"What *is* this place?" He was desperate.

"It's a place...for redemption," she said, as if deciding that it was just that. She seemed to be more hopeful than sure, he thought.

The smoke was overpowering now. He cupped his hands around his mouth and breathed slowly. "We have to get out of here!"

"There's no fire," Victoria said. She sounded neither worried nor sympathetic.

But Alistair could hear the flames now. "Victoria, we have to leave. This place is burning down!"

Without concern, Victoria began winding her music box. It shuddered to life, and again the green light appeared. "You can leave here if you like, Alistair. On *one* condition."

He took a step toward her. "Yes, okay, whatever you say, we just need to get out of here!"

Ignoring his panic, she continued to wind the music box. "You can make things right. Only I can give you that chance." She seemed to be resigned to this, her burden.

"What do you want me to do?" He was frantic. Smoke billowed all around them now. It was becoming hard to breathe. Couldn't she see what was happening? "Just tell me what you want me to do!"

She looked at him then. Alistair could see the fire in her eyes. A single tear welled up, spilled over, and ran down her face. She turned the handle on the music box once more and, as it began to play, said, "Save them."

\* \* \*

It all came rushing at him at once. The fire. The screams. His escape through the woods as the trees on the edges of the campground had ignited. He'd turned to look back just in time to see Velma, carrying The Torso, collapse in flames. He could hear the others. He had thought, then, that he would always hear the sounds of their screaming.

\* \* \*

Alistair stared at the matchbook in his hands. Had that always been there? The flames and smoke were gone. He and Victoria stood in the empty basement.

"Am I trapped here? Forever?"

"You can make this right," Victoria said.

He knew what she was asking of him.

"And let Octavio have them? Let him have everything? Let that scoundrel finally beat me? They're mine! He was always jealous of me! He had Mother fooled. He had all his teachers fooled. He even had Father fooled, in the end. Do you know they left him the farm? He's rich! They left me with nothing! He's gotten everything! Everything! He won't have them. I'd rather die!"

Alistair was out of breath. For a moment, there was only silence. The music box glowed. Victoria hugged it to herself.

"Do you know what you've done?" she asked, but she was already fading. Alistair watched as her image turned to smoke and began to disappear. The darkness of the room filled the space where she'd been. Her green eyes remained the longest, long enough to fix Alistair one last time in their ghostly stare. "You'll live here now," she said. Her voice was all around him. "You'll stay here with your choices. Forever."

He chased after her, knowing it was useless but needing to try. She was gone before he could reach her. Suddenly the room lit up. He spun around, taking it all in. Victoria was gone. He was trapped here. He could see now that he was in a small cement box of a room. No door. No windows. Two chairs were against the wall to his right. Between them was a table. A deck of cards sat on the table, a bottle of wine next to those. He crossed the room, picking up the bottle. It was covered in dust. The greasy duck from the night before sat rotting on a plate. Had it been there a moment ago? It stared at him with one black eye. Alistair uncorked the wine and took a swig, keeping his eye on the carcass.

Just as he began contemplating an eternity in this place, a voice spoke from behind him.

"Hello, brother."

The Second Story: Cruelty / Anger / Hate

# The Barren
## by Meg Hafdahl

Savannah expertly positioned the plastic stick beneath her. Through the ragged, hypnotic haze of her lingering nightmares, she coached herself to pee.

"Come on," she whispered to her bladder.

Finally, she doused the stick, as well as the edge of her right thumb. Savannah flushed the toilet, pulling up her linen pajama pants and then setting the urine-soaked rectangle on the ceramic lip of the sink.

Tingling hope tickled up her sides as she washed her hands with mounds of foamy soap. Her eyes flitted down to the pregnancy test, which still displayed the electronic image of an hourglass.

That physical manifestation of hope intensified. It gripped every muscle, causing Savannah to shiver. She concentrated on drying her hands on the buttercream yellow towel, her internal dialogue a flurry of contradictions.

*This could be it. This could be the time.*

*Don't get excited! It'll only hurt you! It'll take another piece of you. Keep it together, Savannah.*

She pursed her lips, breathing steadily as she stared into the mirror. Her ebony curls were a wild, matted mess. Although she tried to keep her eyes on the eruption of fine new lines at the bridge of her nose, her rebellious eyeballs shifted south.

NOT PREGNANT

The two stark words were a sharp, sudden disruption to her bubble of hope. Despair returned, as it did every month. Savannah staggered back from the cruel rejection, fighting the tears that obscured her sight.

Kenji entered the open bathroom door, mid-yawn. He blinked at Savannah, his dark lashes heavy with sleep. "Okay?"

She managed a pained whimper, curling in on herself as she crumpled to the icy tile.

Her husband knelt at her side, wearing the same mask of detached concern he always did. "Negative?" He squeezed her thigh.

"Why?" Her pain had become anger, simmering hot. "Why me?"

Kenji sighed. "It's going to happen. It's just a matter of time." His indefatigable optimism burned a hole through her heart.

Savannah pressed her chin to her knees, overcome with a quiet, seething rage.

He gave her a sympathetic pat on the shoulder and stood. "Someday we'll look on all this like it was a dream. We'll have a kid, a couple of kids, and we won't even remember all the…bullshit." Kenji made it worse with his assurances, with his casual rake of fingers through his thick hair.

She had never felt so alone. Drowning in a pitch-black well of grief, struggling to a surface that wasn't there, that wouldn't reveal itself to her. There was no pinprick of light, no hope. There was only her, alone: an empty, childless husk.

Savannah made it to the clinic on time. She swiped the badge on the end of her lanyard across the digital lock.

"Dr. Hascomb went to Jamaica." Yvette spoke around the green Starbucks straw between her lips.

"Lucky." Savannah sighed as they passed together into the narrow employee-access hall.

Yvette took a long, gurgling sip of iced coffee. "We're stuck with his overflow, remember?"

"Shit." The fierce hangover of the morning's disappointment had muddied Savannah's thoughts. "That's right. It's going to be a long day."

"Forget lunch break. Dr. Schmidt is going to push through, knowing her." Yvette's camo messenger bag rocked with the motion as she elbowed open the door into the dim waiting room.

Savannah switched on the fluorescent lights. She blinked at the austere room of grey and cream, unable to see anything but her own despair.

"Morning!" Dr. Schmidt trilled from behind them. "Hope you ate your Wheaties today, we're picking up Fred's slack."

Yvette tossed her cup in the trash by the reception desk. "He better bring me back a sparkly souvenir."

"I wouldn't hold my breath, Yvette." Dr. Schmidt, effortlessly beautiful, and the mother of twin toddler girls, fiddled with the crumpled collar of her white coat.

Savannah closed her eyes, allowing herself to hover in the middle of the waiting room. She wondered what sort of morning her boss had experienced. Had she dressed her girls in matching tights and polka-dot blouses? Had she fed them equal amounts of yogurt and fruit in lilac bowls? Had she thanked the universe for her incredible luck? Even Yvette had sixteen-year-old Bucky, who came by the clinic every now and then to drop off McDonalds, or ask her for an advance on his allowance.

Savannah's eyelids popped open. Her visceral rage had torn a painful, burning hole in her stomach. Her usual appetite for coffee had drained away, leaving her both tired and nauseous.

"Okay?" Petite Yvette climbed up onto her towering chair behind the reception desk.

Savannah forced a nod. "Yeah. I'll get the door." She moved toward the glass as though in a dream, questioning the unreality of the morning. Despite the predictably drab clinic and the normal banter of her coworkers, it was difficult to accept the NOT PREGNANT that had stolen her happiness.

A woman waited outside the Hascomb & Schmidt Clinic door, sun streaming across her tanned ankles. Savannah concentrated on the glint of light, how it played across the stranger's expensive leather pumps.

She pulled down on one bolt with her right hand, while loosening another with her left. When she yanked the door open, the waiting woman whisked inside, peppering Savannah with a fragrant cloud of floral perfume.

"Good morning." Savannah kept her eyes on the thin carpet. It was all she could do to focus on being human. To walk, to breathe, to keep her emotions inside like bubbling vomit that threatened to escape, would be the most she could manage.

"Hello." The woman's swollen belly cast a shadow on the carpet. "Hot as hell out there, and it's only eight a.m."

Savannah's ears burned hot at the obvious attack on her already shriveled psyche. Of course the first patient of the day was largely pregnant. She worked to produce a response. "Uh-huh. Scorcher."

"OH!" The woman squeaked.

Savannah glanced up – she was nearly a foot shorter – at the sound. The woman's aristocratic, tawny nose caught at something in the shadowy corridor of her memory.

"You're Savvy! Savvy Chan!"

"Yes." Savannah's brows knit together. "Yamamoto, now." She struggled to make the connection.

"Ferris High! Class of '06!" The woman reached out, her sparkly charm bracelet clacking against Savannah's shoulder as she squeezed the flesh. "Don't you remember me?"

Savannah's nostrils flared at the potent perfume. She studied the woman's face, and the length of her tanned, extended arm, flecked with several dark moles. Their distinct, uneven borders finally ripped open her mind. "Mackenzie Burton." The name fizzled in her chest.

"*Yes!*" Mackenzie dug her manicured nails deeper into Savannah's shoulder. "It's been *ages!* I didn't know you worked here!"

"Hmm." The dull ache of her rage frothed into a palpably bitter taste on her tongue. "You're expecting."

Mackenzie dropped her hand, rubbing the taut fabric of her maternity dress with both palms. "It's number four! Can you believe it?"

Savannah forced her most aggressive fake grin. Her gums grew dry.

"Fertile Myrtle is what Giovanni calls me! That's my husband. He's an orthopedic surgeon over at St. Luke's," Mackenzie boasted.

Mackenzie Burton hadn't changed much since Ferris High. She'd spoken with the same haughty tone back then, quick to point out Savannah's cheap shoes or throbbing pimple, and always to a group of vile, tittering girls.

Savannah could sense her memories of that dark, disappointing time threatening to overtake her. She concentrated on the ripple of baby beneath Mackenzie's dress. It moved visibly, presumably adjusting its cramped limbs.

"Oh!" Mackenzie giggled. The high, shrill pitch nearly transported Savannah to 2006, to the freshly waxed tiles of Ferris High School. "He's a mover and a shaker, I tell you!"

"Congratulations," Savannah offered weakly.

"Thank you! You're a nurse here, then?"

"Yes. Mostly for Dr. Schmidt."

"Ah." Mackenzie swiped a blonde strand of hair away from her lashes. "I'm a patient of Dr. Hascomb. Although I hear the bastard is on a beach somewhere!" She honked.

"Who goes to Jamaica in the summer?" Yvette added from her post at the reception desk.

Mackenzie huffed. "Right!"

Savannah hovered, unable to unglue her eyes from her former classmate's corpulent tummy.

"Yamamoto. You married Kenji? I remember him; quiet, but cheery."

The anger had become black, poisonous sludge. It travelled slowly through Savannah's body like syrup, coating her veins and filling her with sinister notions.

"Kenji Yamamoto?" Mackenzie repeated.

30

"Oh." Savannah ran a trembling hand over the neck of her fuchsia scrubs. "Yes, after college."

"High school sweethearts! I think I remember you two at prom. Remember that shit show? What a lark, trying to coordinate five hundred teenagers on a ferry boat!"

Savannah shrugged.

"How many kids?"

NOT PREGNANT

She glanced down at her flat belly, considering a lie. But Yvette could hear, and that would inevitably get messy. "None...yet."

"It's a blessing." Mackenzie bent her head, eerily, in the same pseudo-show of concern she'd demonstrated when Savannah had slipped on the snowy path outside Ferris and broken her collarbone. "You won't regret it. My children are my reason for living."

A cavernous, awkward silence filled the room.

"Mrs. Burton-Rossi," Yvette interjected. "Dr. Schmidt is ready to see you. I just need to scan your insurance card quick."

Mackenzie nodded, rifling through her pristine Coach purse. "Right away!" She pulled out a slim wallet. "It was nice seeing you, Savvy."

"Uh-huh." The hateful sludge slowed its nauseating course. It cemented itself in Savannah's heart. She bit down on her bottom lip, tasting blood.

In the handicapped-accessible bathroom, with a sliding half-door for urine sample collection, Savannah allowed her jelly legs to crumple. The cool tile floor reminded her of her apartment's bathroom, where she'd spent an inordinate amount of time lately.

A fresh wave of anger had joined her agony. It was the time capsule of her teenaged horror, cracked like an egg and left to ooze.

Mackenzie Burton had been an archetypal bully: the sort of beautiful, marginally clever girl who populated bad teen movies. Yet she'd been real. She had punctuated Savannah's young life with pointed sighs and pitying eye rolls.

And she'd returned, baby straining beneath her belly, to flaunt her gifts. To remind Savannah, years later, that some people have all the luck. That whether she was Savvy Chan or Savannah Yamamoto, LPN, she would have nothing more than a dusty womb full of tumbleweeds.

Savannah bit into the sensitive seam on her lip, licking at the iron. The visceral image of her insides, of a desert with no oasis, formed into something more ominous. She saw the sharp edges of her nightmare. A scalpel expertly navigated through another's soft flesh. Blood and slippery viscera lapped at her feet like the touch of a foamy sea.

It was her own hands, in her mind's eye, working out the prize. The pearl from the oyster. Savannah watched herself pull out the diaphanous sack from the waterfall of blood. She carefully pierced the placenta, widening an opening in order to see. To meet her baby.

It had stark black hair, like Kenji.

Savannah gulped in air, drunk with the possibility of it all happening so soon.

*Now. Today.*

She could be a mother today. She could hear her baby's cry, feel the bottoms of its wrinkled feet, smell its unique and intoxicating aroma.

It was only Mackenzie who stood in the way. Pompous, cruel, fertile Mackenzie.

In the fervor of her daydream, Savannah remembered the baby's ripple beneath the thin fabric of Mackenzie's dress.

It was so achingly close.

Now, as she rubbed at the thread of blood on her chin, Savannah understood that the baby had been calling to her.

*Hi, Momma. I'm here, Momma. I'm ready to come home.*

The sounds of the busy clinic burrowed their way into Savannah's ears. Dr. Schmidt laughed about something near her office at the end of the hall. Mackenzie joined in, her braying giggle upsetting the last shred of Savannah's umbilicus to reality.

She concentrated on the smudge of blood on her palm, understanding.

If she navigated through the rage, if she let the molten-hot fire lead her rather than burn her, Savannah could be a mother today.

\* \* \*

It was easy to find Mackenzie's chart. Savannah calmly clicked the mouse hovering over the red tab, hitting PRINT PAGE ONE before Yvette could look up from her paperwork and glance at the screen.

The single page came out warm. Savannah cradled it, absorbing the address written above Mackenzie's weight and height.

"What a bitch," Yvette snorted under her breath.

Startled, Savannah folded the paper, stuffing it into the manila folder containing Mr. Armando's prescription instructions. "Hmm?"

"Sorry if she's your friend, but that blonde pregnant lady is hard to take." Yvette spoke through her synthetic smile, plastered on for the benefit of those filling the waiting room.

Savannah hugged the folder to her chest. "Always was." The certainty of her convictions straightened her back. It raised her shoulders and lifted her chin. This was what needed to be done. This was what it would take.

"Typical."

"I'm going for a walk."

Yvette looked up from a note written in Dr. Schmidt's scraggily script. "Huh?"

"I need some air. I'm sick or something."

"You do look a bit pale." Yvette wrinkled her wide nose. "I can cover for you."

"Thanks." Savannah turned her back to Yvette in order to slip the paper into the waistband of her scrub pants. She dropped Mr. Armando's papers on the desk and headed for the glittering call of the outdoors. On her way to the glass door, the patients-- and the tables smattered with magazines--took on an abstraction in her mind. She was surrounded by only shapes and colors, encapsulated by a crushing tunnel of things that no longer mattered.

As soon as the muggy summer air whooshed through the strands of her ebony hair, Savannah felt better. She strode to the curb, breathing mindfully through her nostrils. The paper scratched at the skin of her hip. It was a pleasant irritation, one that reminded her of the task at hand. Of the integral nature of her decision, of her purpose.

Savannah crossed Valley View Avenue, her eyes glued to the brick side of the mini-mall. Someone honked, but it was tinny and inconsequential. She shook her head, following the sloped parking lot to her destination.

Valley Mall was an old-fashioned structure with ten storefronts connected by a roofed sidewalk. Savannah passed Rooster's Grill, her favorite lunch place with Yvette, and Sally's Fabric and Craft, maneuvering around the obstacles of people. She began to count her steps, each one punctuated by the rustle of the paper against the thin fabric of her underwear.

The Ace Hardware's door was held open by a thick Rubbermaid filled with pool noodles and squirt guns. Savannah nearly tripped over the summer goodies as she entered the shop.

"'Morning." A man, only a brown and blue shape in her periphery, greeted Savannah as she rushed toward the tools. "Looking for something in particular?"

She extended her finger, carefully touching the toothed edge of a hacksaw. "I'm fine." For the first time since she'd pushed through the clinic door, she wasn't sure that was true. It occurred to her, as she lifted the saw up from its hook, that she might not have it in her. That what it took to be a mother today might be too high a price.

*Back away, Savannah. Stop. This is nuts.*

A voice, similar to her own, echoed.

*Momma, I'm waiting for you. I'm here, Momma.*

At the thought of her baby, trapped inside Mackenzie, the weakness drained away. Her limbs tingled with the certainty of her mission. Savannah grabbed the hacksaw, a utility knife, and a folded tarp.

She dropped her bounty on the shop counter.

The faceless man slowly punched numbers into the old-fashioned till. He might have spoken about the weather, but Savannah was too tangled in the web of her sharp thoughts to be sure. A vague paranoia of being found out, of being caught and ultimately stopped, threatened to overshadow the excitement of her plan.

After paying with the credit card in her scrubs' pocket, Savannah nodded a thank you. She swung the plastic bag of tools against her thigh as she stepped back out into the muggy day. Sweat erupted on her top lip. She licked at the salt, nearly blinded by the intense sunlight. A bench beneath the feeble shade of the roofed sidewalk called to her.

Savannah slumped onto the wooden slats, staring back at the window display of sprinklers at Ace Hardware. She was keenly aware of Mackenzie's address, now a bit soggy, curled at her hip. She settled the plastic bag beside her, unable to think of anything else but the end result. Her baby. Her baby wrapped in a sweet blanket. Kenji would be thrilled!

An amorphous woman walked by, her flip-flops slapping the cement. Savannah smiled at the distinctive shopping bag in the woman's grip.

It was from the baby store, Tina's Tiny Treasures, at the far end of Valley Mall. It had been a place Savannah actively avoided, a reminder of her failures. Of an alternate life she had been too weak to fight for.

Not now. Not anymore.

Savannah rested a hand on her wet brow, peering over at where Tina's Tiny Treasures would undoubtedly have their tented chalkboard. It would say something clever like *splash into summer with our newborn swim gear!*

She squinted, unable to make out the pink gingham curtains. The chalkboard wasn't there either, or the painted, life-sized Elmo that waved mothers in.

Leaning forward, Savannah noticed a comforting shadow blocking the sun's assault. It darkened the edge of the sidewalk, casting a cool reprieve across her legs, and then her entire body.

Fear stole her breath. The piercing, intrusive script of her thoughts stuttered. Savannah stood, disbelieving.

Tina's Tiny Treasures had been leveled. In its stead was a towering building, fused haphazardly to the Subway that shared a wall with the hardware store.

Savannah concentrated on the strange patched-together seam between the sandwich shop and the ancient-looking structure.

"Tina's Treasures?" she squeaked. The question fizzled in the heavy air, making her wonder if she was speaking inside a dream.

The empty sidewalk grew cool. Blood rushed to Savannah's ears as a summer breeze shifted the pool noodles outside Ace. She moved toward the impossible building, clutching her purchases beneath her odorous armpit. It was old and, at the same time, new.

She'd have noticed such a blight before, surely. Yet here it was, stories higher than the squat mini-mall. Its windows were black, taunting mouths.

Savannah found herself drawn to the peculiarly sentient edifice. A meek piece of her consciousness wondered where Tina's Tiny Treasures had gone, and if this meant she would have to buy her new baby's clothes at the Super Target.

The throbbing forefront of her mind studied the building's classical lines. It bothered her how it was obviously from long ago: beautiful, and designed with an architectural eye, but it had been crudely glued to the side of an artless, shoebox-like Subway.

The incongruity ate at her as she found herself stepping further into the cool, enveloping shadow of the behemoth.

"Hello?" A voice, young and curious, distracted Savannah from the sneering lip of an awning above the front door.

"Yes?" Savannah answered back with a question, her mind fuzzy from the confounding building and, more, from the feel of the sharp tools beneath her arm.

A girl held the door open with her skinny elbow. "You're looking for the baby shop." She spoke with a precocious accent.

"Yes! Where's it gone?" Savannah's eyes finally focused on the small blonde girl. "It was here last week."

*It was here a few moments ago.* The voice deep within, the same one that begged her to set down the saw and run away from the hardware store, bubbled up. *There was a woman walking by, holding a Tina's Tiny Treasures shopping bag. How does that make sense, Savvy?*

That nickname brought an image of Mackenzie, rotund and insincere. Anger caused red polka dots to stipple Savannah's sight.

"They've closed, I'm afraid. Permanently." The girl motioned inside with her porcelain chin. "You're coming in, aren't you?"

"I'm busy." Savannah panted, hearing the crinkling of the plastic bag at her side. She knew if she didn't go through with all of this now, the voice inside would get louder, and it would only work to question her. To prevent her from getting what she so desperately wanted, and what Mackenzie, it was clear, deserved.

The girl with the blonde ringlets was eaten up by the door. She disappeared into the darkness as it creaked on rusted hinges. Perplexed as to why she'd given up on her so easily, Savannah followed.

It was twenty degrees cooler, maybe more, than the Valley Mall lot. Savannah's eyes adjusted to the damp darkness. Her nostrils wiggled at the unmistakable scent of must. Goosebumps etched their way up her arms, ending at the short sleeves of her scrub top.

"My name's Victoria." The girl leaned casually against a wall tattooed with mildewed wallpaper. "Not that what we call ourselves really matters. I could say I'm Edith or George and it wouldn't make a whit of difference, would it, Savannah?"

Savannah bit down on the sensitive part of her lip, where'd she drawn blood earlier. This girl, Victoria, she was like the building. An old thing, haphazardly stuck to a new thing. Her formal hairstyle, and her velvet dress with puff sleeves, was wholly wrong.

"And you know her name, don't you?" The girl patted at something cradled in her arms.

"Huh?"

"Remember?"

Savannah's gaze dropped from Victoria's strangely wise face down to the item she carried.

The baby doll's bald head and pink, gummy smile forced Savannah to stumble back. She goggled at the impossible. It was more unbelievable than a building that sprouted from the ether.

"It's Donna." She bit harder at the familiar sight, tasting metal. Donna, her Cabbage Patch Doll, the very one she'd walked around the neighborhood in a cheap plastic baby carriage. The one she'd rocked, and "fed," and dressed.

It had been her own small hands that had put on the striped pink sleep sack that Donna wore as she rested her head on Victoria's arm.

An elevator dinged behind the girl holding Savannah's prized childhood possession. All three of them made their way inside the confining lift in a surreal, quiet haze.

Savannah supposed Victoria pushed a button, but she was too transfixed by the doll to even notice the door closing. "Did you steal her?"

Victoria giggled, clutching the Cabbage Patch Doll tighter.

The elevator trundled up, its vibrations waking Savannah from her momentary paralysis. She grabbed at Donna, swiftly removing her baby doll from the girl's pale hands. The plastic hardware store bag plummeted to the floor with a clang.

"Oh!" With a grin, Victoria stood back.

Savannah pushed her thumbs into the baby's soft middle, and then caressed her cold bald head.

Donna had been a part of the "Preemie Collection," smaller than most Cabbage Patch Dolls. Touching her, feeling her weight, triggered a fresh seepage of rage.

"You stole her! From my things!" Savannah couldn't remember where and when she'd last seen Donna. Had it been a decade, in the cramped attic bedroom that had once been hers? Or had Donna come to the apartment she shared with Kenji, tucked away in a box with old Polaroids and long-ago art projects? Whatever the case, this strange girl in the formal dress had taken her.

"Here we are." Victoria waggled her thin blonde brows at the elevator doors opening at floor number two.

Savannah concentrated on Donna's synthetic eyes. The earnest nature of the painted irises made her at once furious and melancholy. Her feet moved her off the lift and onto the second floor, while her brain only worked to understand the doll in her grip.

"You disapprove of stealing?" Victoria asked.

"Of course."

Victoria swung the Ace Hardware bag Savannah had dropped. It thwacked her against her little thigh. "Unless it's justified? Unless a person truly deserves the object?"

Savannah glanced up from Donna's perpetual, gummy smile. "I don't know what you–" She slammed her jaw shut.

Where she stood, it was like Tina's Tiny Treasures, only better.

A row of magnificent cribs stretched down either side of the endless corridor. Each one was different: mahogany, rustic timber, gold-flecked ivory. Breathless, Savannah marveled at the beauty.

Surrounding each crib was a tableau of what could be. There were rocking chairs; side tables with diaper holders of many colors; rugs; toys; and bookshelves decorated with pewter bears.

Like a hapless component of an electrical charge, she was drawn to the pretty things, the things she always wanted but never seemed to have. For it was women like Mackenzie, like Dr. Schmidt, or like Yvette who could have babies. Not her.

Not her.

As though to accentuate this point, Victoria stood beside Savannah and patted her empty womb with her tiny palm. "There's something growing inside of you."

"Shut up." Savannah swatted Victoria's hand away, nearly losing hold of Donna.

"It's ugly," Victoria continued. "It's the opposite of what you want. It's all the bad ideas and mean, putrid thoughts, Savannah."

Savannah chewed on the bloody meat of her inner lip. "You don't know. You have no idea how badly it hurts." A physical pain shot through her abdomen.

The little girl paced, finally resting her arm on an oak crib. "You hate her."

"Mackenzie."

"She was cruel to you in high school."

"Yes." Savannah sniffled. That voice within rose up, begging an explanation for this madness. She swatted it down, unwilling to question the beauty of the room.

"She's haughty. Spoiled. Immature."

Savannah nodded, her eyes trailing the intricate design of the bird-themed wallpaper behind Victoria.

"And she's a mother."

This forced a thorn into Savannah's heart. She took in a shaking breath. "Of three! With another on the way!"

Victoria cocked her head. "It's not fair."

Blood coated Savannah's tongue. She bit through the pain, pleased at the taste. "She wouldn't even care, or notice…"

The oak crib with the giraffe mobile and cheetah-printed bumper called to her. Savannah reached out, touching the railing with a single finger.

Victoria stepped away, allowing Savannah to wrap her hand around the top rail. It was real. It was solid. "You were going to use the saw."

Savannah stared at one of the soft yellow giraffes. "I don't want to hurt anyone."

*That's a lie.* It was that voice, always there, lurking in the corners of her soul. *You want to hurt her, to make her suffer. For being a "Fertile Myrtle," for being a brat, for being a mother.*

"You were going to cut Mackenzie open, to get what you think you deserve." Victoria finished the stream of thoughts.

For the first time, Savannah admitted to herself that this was true. She'd only allowed herself fragmented ideas, but now, she could finally see the entirety of her plan.

At this, the weight in her arms changed. She looked down to find Donna had disappeared. Instead, there was the hacksaw, wrapped in a soft baby-blue blanket. Savannah gasped at its menacing teeth.

The giraffe mobile began to spin. It played a lazy, warbled rendition of *You Are My Sunshine*.

Trembling, she dared to step closer to the crib, pressing her belly against the rails. The hacksaw slipped from her arms, sliding to the clapboard floor.

Entranced by what she would find, Savannah peered down into the crib. The vibrant crimson of dried blood caught her eye. It was smeared against the cloth bumper sides, and stippled across the jungle-themed comforter. A lifeless lump was visible beneath the gore. Nausea mixed with the deep well of anger as she slowly pulled the blanket.

*You've done this. You're responsible.*

She wasn't sure if it was her own inner voice, or that of Victoria.

And it didn't matter.

Savannah's hands shook violently as she yanked the final inches off, revealing the blood-soaked head of an infant. Rivulets of red trailed down into the familiar pseudo-eyes.

"No!" Savannah grabbed Donna, naked and tacky with blood, from the mattress. She clutched the doll to her chest, nearly drowning in her own grief and rage.

"There's something growing inside of you." It was undeniably Victoria, yet she spoke from far away, as if over a loudspeaker.

Savannah staggered back, her eyes adjusting to her new reality. The rows of cribs filtered away, giving form to the sterile, hollow hall of a hospital. It was the hazy, incomplete set change of a dream.

"Hello?" Her voice echoed down the linoleum paved corridor. "Where'd you go?"

"Desperation turns to sadness, and sadness turns to anger," Victoria boomed. "If you don't stop, Savannah, it will grow larger."

"*Hello*?" Savannah screeched, eager to find another human being. She raced down the hall, her sneakers squeaking on the waxed floor. Every room, even the nurses' station, was empty. "*Please*?" She stopped in what looked like a waiting room, one stocked with magazines displaying bright pictures of cherubic babies.

Something rippled inside of her.

It was unlike any sensation she'd felt before.

It was as if her body wasn't her own.

Savannah rested a hand on the top of her belly, shocked to discover it had taken on a new, rotund shape. She set Donna carefully down on a chair, and then returned both hands to her alien stomach. It grew by the second, straining the tight hem of her scrub top and stretching her pants to their max.

"Oh my God." She was...it was too wonderful, too perfect to be true.

*POP!* Her belly button audibly jutted out, while stretch marks carved uneven lines on her sides.

Then it moved, twisting her insides, and creating a bizarre ripple at the base of her enormous abdomen.

"*Oh!*" She reveled in the feel. Tears muddied her vision as she desperately searched for its return against her skin.

The scrub pants cut into her flesh. Savannah slipped them off. A piece of paper flitted to the floor. She removed her top next, instantly greeted by a swollen pair of breasts that spilled over the cups of her bra.

Had she willed this to be?

Had she wanted a baby so ardently that the universe was providing?

"Savannah." Victoria sounded worried. Savannah couldn't help but notice the strain in the little girl's tone. "You have to decide. You have to let the anger subside, let it go...otherwise, oh..." The crackling fizzle of the hospital's loudspeaker cut out.

Savannah proudly massaged her massive belly. Her inner voice was trying to say something, but she'd muzzled it.

Suddenly a *whoosh* of liquid sloshed at her sneakers. She glanced down at the clear fluid, the nurse side of her waking at the immediacy of what had happened. Savannah touched her bare wet thigh, realizing she was in labor. Alone.

A walloping pain stole her breath, causing her to sink her nails into the soft wood of a chair's arm. "*Ahhhh*!"

"The anger, Savannah, is holding you back. It made you think those things today, make those vile plans." Victoria's voice filled the howling void of Savannah's mind.

Savannah fell to her knees, grasping at her pained middle. "*Help*!"

"Help yourself!" Victoria insisted.

"*I need help*!" Savannah roared.

In nursing school, Savannah had witnessed many women in labor. She'd wondered what it might feel like a million times, but this wasn't what she'd expected. Blood, black and viscous, pooled beneath her. She was sure the baby inside, the thing, was eating its way out with razor teeth.

Every nerve in her body was on fire, the pain ratcheting up when she thought it wasn't possible to hurt anymore.

Savannah tried, weakly, to crawl toward a hospital room, but her legs gave out in the bloodied muck. She flipped onto her back, trying to focus on the square tiles of the ceiling. Her vision waxed and waned, threatening to desert her.

Drumbeats of rhythmic pain shook her entire frame. Savannah whimpered, wishing she had Kenji, or anyone, who could whisper refreshing axioms in her ear and assure her this was natural.

But although she'd never carried a baby in her belly, Savannah knew this wasn't the way of things.

The pain that blossomed inside of her was a different animal, a blistering pimple with only sludge to expel.

She curled onto her side and, through the agony, could make out Victoria's patent leather shoes and frilled socks.

The little girl knelt at Savannah's side, her eyes more sincere and empathetic than Donna's could ever be. "Release yourself." She gently stroked Savannah's sweaty cheek.

"*Uhhh!*" Savannah moaned, knowing that this fight had changed. She couldn't let what churned inside of her free. In its exodus, it would rip her apart. Her legs clanged together instinctively.

"It's not fair." She cried hot, fat tears. "It's not…" She held her breath, ignoring the urge to bear down and push the lava from within. "It's not fair that Mackenzie, that…anyone gets to be a mother. *But not me!*" The anger, the fear, the frustration overwhelmed the pain, and then twisted itself into what was even more excruciating: an unfathomable sadness.

"You're wrong," Victoria soothed. "It shouldn't matter what we call ourselves, but it does."

"*Ahh!*" A seam of fire seemed to work its way through Savannah's middle. She leaned her head back, the ends of her black hair glossing through the putrid blood.

Victoria grasped her hand. "Savannah, you *are* a mother. You have been since the day you got Donna, do you remember?"

Savannah let out wisps of air from pursed lips, feeling as if the abandoned hospital was now on a

49

rollicking ship in a hurricane. The walls vibrated. "What?"

"Do you remember?" Victoria repeated.

Savannah closed her dry eyelids, navigating through the intense pain. It had been her birthday, hot and sweaty just like today. Donna had been wrapped in mint-green tissue paper. When Savannah had seen her, smiling and silently asking to be loved, she knew. Knew she was meant to be a mother. The good, warm, happy sort of mother who was born to it.

An incredible sense of purpose burrowed its way into her tortured mind. She found the strength to sit up, to take in a long, lasting breath. "I lost myself."

"Yes!" Victoria tapped her feet in the gore.

"It's...it's not about fair."

The little girl nodded.

Savannah realized the pain was subsiding. The top of her belly deflated slowly, like a pool float stuck with a slender pin.

"I *am* a mother."

The sharp fragments of her rage splintered. She was left with only the purpose. Not of cribs and music mobiles, but of something else.

Dressed in her soiled underwear, Savannah stood up in the sticky pool of her anger. "I *am* a mother."

"What will you do about it?" Victoria pointed to the chair where Donna waited, clean and dressed in her sleep sack. Beside her sat the hacksaw, wrapped in its blanket.

Ashamed of how desperate, how angry, she'd become, Savannah hung her head.

*Not that.*

The voice became Savannah's. "Not that."

She wasn't certain how she got back on the sidewalk, or how her scrubs were placed on her clean body, yet she was standing in the oppressive sun. Donna, Victoria, the building, and her bag from Ace Hardware had all left her.

Alone.

Savannah squinted at the assault of light, rubbing her flat stomach with her palm.

She noticed that while the building had disappeared from its temporary place beside Subway, Tina's Tiny Treasures hadn't returned.

The structure was the same, a utilitarian square, yet it had a new sign in the window. In fact, a woman with brilliant copper hair and a tattoo of a giraffe on her freckled arm was affixing the final letter to the glass.

"Tina's?" Savannah asked.

"Moved over to the Arlendale Plaza, I think?" The woman stepped down off a stepstool, taking in her work.

"Oh, all right," Savannah muttered, still trapped in the whirlwind of what she'd just endured and what she'd nearly been driven to do.

"How's it look? Straight, I hope?"

Savannah took a few paces back to read the words:

SOUTHWEST METRO CHILD ADOPTION SERVICES

She trembled. "It's straight."

The woman gave an exhausted sigh. "Thanks! It's hot as all get out!"

"Uh-huh." Savannah lingered, thinking of Donna, who, she was now sure, she'd donated to a charity drive years earlier.

The woman raised an eyebrow. "We open next Tuesday."

"Okay."

"Would you like a pamphlet?"

"Yes." Savannah smoothed down the front of her billowing scrub top. "Yes, I would." An emptiness filled within her. It was as though she was suddenly brimming with an indefinable emotion--something, she guessed, a lot like hope.

The Third Story: Theft

# Raising Change
## by Jon Grilz

The air was hot and dry. The wind swelled around him in bursts, filled with dust, cologne, and more than a few other scents Joe didn't appreciate. He looked up at the lights, a massive LED display of Chester from Linkin Park playing overhead as tribute. The crowd paused, pointed their cameras up, sang along to the songs they knew. Joe kept moving. He walked past the massive row of daiquiri machines, their constant slow tumble of sugar and booze enticing the already drunken masses to shell out another $20 for what amounted to a waste of money.

Joe knew what brought him there to that moment, wandering alone down Fremont Street, but he couldn't figure out why. Not entirely. The spur-of-the-moment decision felt like the right thing to do. It went against his instincts. It was rash and bold. It was as far from his life at home as he could get on a limited budget and short notice.

Fuck her.

A ring clinked against some spare change in his left jeans pocket. He took it off at the airport security check, dropping it into the bin with the change as he

54

waited to get scanned. As he pulled his phone, wallet, shoes, and belt out of the bin on the other end, he tilted the bin to retrieve the change, but he let the ring get lost.

As he walked, his left thumb still found the small dent just above the knuckle on his ring finger and rubbed at the smooth skin.

A heavily-bearded man, dressed as a demon and standing on foot-tall boot lifts, waved a goathead scepter around to the amusement of the masses, bellowing, posing for pictures, shilling himself for money to be dropped into his bucket. Joe didn't know that was a part of the experience. The last time he'd been in Vegas was for his brother's excessively awkward bachelor party. They'd stayed on the strip, and the most they'd dealt with on the street were the rows of Mexicans slapping up ads for escorts.

It was all weird.

With his attention otherwise diverted, Joe barely noticed the impact into his right shoulder. He spun to reflexively apologize, but another voice rose above the music.

"Oh my God, I'm so sorry." Her green eyes flashed with sincerity and apology so intense that a person would think she'd just hit Joe with her car.

"It's okay," Joe said, brushing it off.

"I'm sorry," she said, her apology fading to a soft smile. "I was trying to avoid those two twerking over there." She pointed back over her shoulder to what were, in fact, two very curvaceous, scantily-clad women shaking their asses for a group of hooting men, all with their phones out, recording the show.

"I don't blame you," Joe said, and started to turn.

A hand on Joe's arm made him pause. The touch was soft, unimposing. "Hey," the woman said, "you wouldn't happen to know where The Underground is, do you?"

Joe looked around. "Sorry, no."

"Oh," the woman said, slightly defeated. She was fairly attractive, but not in the obvious way that a lot of the women in the streets at that moment were. She wore a sundress and had her blonde hair pulled back into a ponytail. She had a Midwestern sort of look, almost like she was constantly ready to apologize about something. "I thought maybe you were from around here."

Joe smirked at the idea of being mistaken for a local. Nothing about him felt local to Vegas. "No, I'm from Milwaukee."

"Bigger city than me," she said. "Hi, I'm Kara."

She held out her hand, and Joe took it in his. "Joe."

"Hi Joe," she said with a silly smirk and an exaggerated pumping motion of her hand, as if she realized the strange nature of their interaction and how awkward they both felt in that moment. It made Joe smile.

Kara released her grip and looked around. "This is all a little overwhelming."

"Yeah," said Joe. "It's something."

"I was supposed to meet my friends at some underground bar. Like, they'd just opened it up and it was all exclusive to people in the know, or whatever people call it."

"I...don't know what people call it," Joe said.

Kara smiled again and held his gaze for a moment. "I don't either...God, this is horribly awkward, isn't it?"

Joe shook his head. "Not more than that guy," he said, pointing to the man walking past in a slingshot bikini and enough body hair to be mistaken for wearing a sweater.

Kara laughed and covered her eyes. "Oh my God."

"Yeah, you can't unsee something like that," Joe said.

They shared another awkward moment, Joe suddenly feeling another flash of uncharacteristic behavior. But before he could get a word out, Kara said something, her voice quiet and lost in the din around them.

"I'm sorry?" he said.

Kara blushed and looked like she wanted to suddenly run away. "No, I'm sorry, that was so stupid."

Joe took a moment to try and trace the conversation backward. "What? No, I meant that I didn't hear what you just asked."

"Oh..." Kara stammered, looking to summon the courage to speak again and dig herself out of whatever hole she thought she was in. "I was just wondering if maybe you wanted to go get a drink. I really don't want to go to some club or whatever. And my friends are jerks, not returning my texts. The concierge at my hotel said there's a bar just a couple blocks over that's a bit more low-key."

That was the moment when the doubt hit. In that flash he believed with absolutely certainty that the woman was a hooker and she was just trying to rope him in. There was no way that a cute woman would suddenly just happen to run into him in the middle of Fremont, hit it off, and ask if he wanted to get a drink. That sort of thing just didn't happen to Joe. It had never happened to Joe. He felt his mood sour.

"Listen, I'm sure you've very nice, and I don't know how this sort of thing usually works, but..." He let the words hang, hoping she would get the message and just excuse herself. He didn't get the reaction he expected.

Her previous awkwardness and embarrassment shifted to a look he could only interpret as disgust. "You think I'm a hooker?"

Not knowing what to say, Joe didn't say anything.

Kara scoffed. "I can't believe this. I hate this city. I try to be nice and ask someone…and you accuse me of being a hooker…" Kara turned to walk away.

Joe's face grew even hotter. He should have let it be. He should have let her go and just filed the instance away in his own private memory vault of embarrassing moments: the sort of thing he would forget until the image randomly came into his head while he drove home from work, years from that moment, and he'd cringe at his behavior and wonder *what if.*

He should have, but he didn't. Instead he reached out and put his hand on Kara's bare shoulder.

She spun quickly, as if being attacked, and Joe defensively put his hands up, hoping to look prostrate in the moment. "I'm so sorry, I didn't mean to imply anything. It's just that, I mean, I just got here, and I don't normally just meet people like this…and…you know…it's Vegas."

All he got in return was a glare that made him a little nervous that a slap was forthcoming.

"So because I'm a woman, and I asked a man I just met to have a drink in Las Vegas, I must be a hooker?"

The words vomited out of Joe's mouth in a stuttered jumble of apologies and bad excuses. Finally, Joe asked if he could make it up to her and at least buy her a drink. "If you're still mad at me when we get there, you can even throw it in my face," he said, feeling suddenly impressed by what he thought to be a charming line.

Whether or not it was, it worked. Kara begrudgingly agreed, and the two walked in near silence to the end of Fremont, turning away from the masses and into a quieter neighborhood, finally ending up at a place that just said "BAR" on the door. Joe's defenses flared up for just a moment again in the moments between when his hand reached for the door and when he stepped inside. He'd expected a dive bar, but it looked more hipster and upscale than anything he could have anticipated.

The space was small, but reasonably filled. The floorspace was minimal, with a few semi-circle couches center around gas-flame fire pits. With even only a few dozen people in the bar, it felt full. Not uncomfortable, but just right. The doorman, dressed all in black, who looked like more door than man (Joe couldn't even begin to guess what size suit he was wearing), checked their IDs at the door, looked them up and down and nonchalantly waved them in.

They sat on two open stools near the end of the bar. They watched as the bartender took his time making a few drinks. The man wore a plaid shirt with a bow tie and suspenders. He had a well-kept beard and slicked-back brown hair, and he took his time making the orders in front of him. Joe wasn't a big fan of mixed drinks; for whatever reason, it seemed like a ridiculous amount of attention got paid to adding really weird ingredients for flare, or whatever. After waiting about five minutes, the bartender finally made his way down.

"What can I get ya?" he asked, resting his hands on the rail.

"Do you…" Joe paused, "…have happy hour or anything?"

"It's always happy hour here," the bartender said without a shred of irony.

"What do you recommend?" Kara asked.

"House old-fashioned. We infuse our own bourbon and make our own bitters."

"Sounds good," Kara said. "Two, please."

The bartender nodded and turned to Joe. "And for you?" he asked with a wry smile, before waving the comment off and going to make the drinks.

They sat there in silence, watching the drinks get made. Joe's knee bounced. Kara made no indication of the mood she was in. As the drinks were finally set in front of them in lowball glasses, Joe broke the silence. "So, are you going to throw that at me?"

Kara lifted her glass and paused, before turning and holding it toward him. "I was thinking about it up until that moment. How about if we just drink them?" The two clicked their glasses together and drank.

And drank.

And drank.

Ten drinks between the two of them in only a couple of hours. Joe's eyes swam. Kara didn't look to be much better off. They laughed and shared stories. Joe avoided talking about the life waiting for him back home, but couldn't help dancing closely to that edge, only pulling back when it felt as if he was going to tell too much. He didn't know where the conversation was heading, but he didn't want it to stop something that might be exactly what he needed in his life.

Eventually, Kara looked at her watch. "Oh geez, I didn't realize how late it was. I need to get going."

"Oh," Joe said in a moment of disappointment.

Kara finished the rest of what was in her glass and shrugged. "I mean, you could come with if you wanted. I'm sure my friends wouldn't mind." She signaled the bartender for the check and opened her purse.

"No, no, this was my idea," Joe said. "I've got this."

"Are you sure?" Kara asked. "We had a lot to drink."

"Please," Joe said.

Kara shrugged. "And they say chivalry is dead. I just need to give my friends a call and find out where they are. Meet me outside?"

"Sounds like a plan," Joe said.

"Don't be long. I'm sure they're already pissed at me for ditching them to come here." Kara stood, pulled her phone from her purse, and walked to the door.

The bartender set the bill in front of Joe. Joe looked at it, but his vision didn't quite catch up, and the blur of numbers made no sense. Too many zeros. He looked at the bill again.

$300.

Joe pulled the receipt closer to his face, sure that it couldn't possibly say that. He flagged down the bartender, unable to completely restrain his desperation. "Excuse me, there's some mistake."

The bartender arched an eyebrow and walked over. He took the receipt and shook his head. "No, no mistake. Ten drinks, twenty-five bucks each, 20% tip added on tabs over $200." He handed the receipt back to Joe and tapped on the bottom of the bill, showing the gratuity clause, then pointed over his shoulder toward a sign above the register that echoed the same sentiment.

"You…you said it was happy hour," Joe said. It was all he could think of at the moment.

"It's a just a turn of phrase, man." The bartender took a step back, looked Joe up and down and let out a sharp whistle. "Hey, Ray, we got a problem over here."

The mass of humanity that sat at the door stood slowly and crossed the floor, creating a massive shadow against the lighting. As the man stopped behind Ray, towering over him, Joe could feel the bass of the man's voice in his teeth. "You a deadbeat?"

Joe shook his head and reached for his wallet, pulling it out and handing over his credit card. The bartender ran the card, handed it back, and stood there with the bouncer, staring at Joe as he signed the bill. Joe didn't bother to say anything as he moved away from the bar and toward the door. He felt a huge hand grip his shoulder.

"Nah," Ray said. "Trash goes out the back, you whiny little bitch."

Ray started to guide Joe toward the back door. Joe started to offer a word of protest, but the drink and fear kept him in check. By the time he figured his way out of the back alley, after what ended up being a full lap around the block to get his bearings and find the front of the bar, Kara was gone. He tried to look in the front door, hoping that maybe she'd gone back inside to look for him, but the bouncer stood at the sight of Joe and just shook his head.

Joe started to shake.

Karl hardly noticed the ding of the door chime anymore. That fucking sound of yet another asshole walking into the store, either drunk or stoned, being an idiot, barely able to figure out how their card went into the reader, then stumbling away. He took solace in it being his last day, but not much. The irritations he'd felt at the job for the last two years weighed heavier with the knowledge he would soon be gone, on to something else. Anything else.

Phones were off-limits during work hours, but what were they going to do, fire him? He pulled his phone from his pocket and scrolled through his contacts until he found his roommate. Whoever had walked in the door had moved over toward the coolers, and looked to be having way too much trouble trying to pick a flavor of iced coffee.

The phone rang once before the other end picked up.

"Sup," Lance said on the other end, in that slow surfer-boy drawl.

"Fuckin' bored, man," Karl said. He swiveled left and right on the stool behind the counter. "Six hours to go before I'm gone for good, and the clock is killing me."

The flick of the lighter on the other end, followed by a slow bubbling noise, made the wait that much harder. After a pause and a cough, Lance croaked out, "Just gotta put it outta your mind, man. Focus on the positive."

"Easy for you to say, you don't have to deal with this shit."

"Come on man, chill, just six more hours and we can party like you got no place to be tomorrow." A pause. "Cuz you don't!" Lance laughed way too hard at his joke, and coughed violently enough that Karl had to pull the phone away from his head. It wasn't until that moment that he noticed the woman had moved from the display case to the counter. She'd clearly had too hard of a time figuring out what to drink, and instead just set a pack of gum on the counter.

"Later, man, gotta go," he said, hanging up the phone and sliding it back into his pocket. He forced a smile, but couldn't suppress a sigh as he asked if that was all for her. He didn't even really look at customers anymore. They all just sort of ran together into a blob of annoyance.

"That's it," she said. She sounded sober, which was strange enough for 2am on a Saturday. Still, he reflexively scanned the gum.

"Dollar even."

The woman reached into her purse and pulled out a ten. Karl's arm reached out without even thinking, took the bill, grabbed the nine dollars in change and handed it back. As his hand moved to close his drawer, he heard a soft, "Wait." The woman took the change, but paused.

"I'm sorry, I just saw that I had a dollar. Could I have that ten back?"

Karl stood, confused for a moment, but more annoyed at the realization that she was probably high and just managed it better than most.

"Sure, whatever," he said, grabbing the ten out of the till and handing it back to her.

She took the ten, and handed both the ones and the ten back to him. "Here. If I give you one more, can I just get a twenty back?"

"Um...yeah..." Karl said, confused at the interaction and why buying a pack of gum had suddenly turned into a math equation. He put the money back into the till and handed over a twenty-dollar bill.

"Thank you so much," the woman said, putting the gum in her pocket, and walked out the door. Karl sat there for a moment, something bothering him about what had just happened, before shrugging the feeling off. Five hours, fifty-eight minutes to go.

\* \* \*

Lisa popped a mint into her mouth as she walked past Ray, setting a fond hand of familiarity on his shoulder.

"Hey girl," he said as Lisa disappeared inside. "He long gone."

Lisa walked to the far side of the bar, where Michael was wiping down a glass. He looked up and nodded, setting a bundle of bills on the counter. He flicked at his mustache as he shook his head. Took three tourists that night, but it was a solid take. That second one was dumb enough to order champagne. She took the bills and added them to her purse before heading out into the warm night.

Lisa didn't make it to Vegas as much as she used to. More security made the cons tougher to run with much regularity. She liked Reno. She liked working Indian reservations and dives, but Vegas was fun for a change of pace; even then, she stayed way off the strip. Even way off Fremont. She liked the hotels; a person might see them, driving to or from the airport, and wonder how they could even exist. Places that were so far off the beaten path that they only had the seriously degenerate gamblers there. Men and women that reeked of desperation. The sorts of mooks who should be better gamblers, but their need to finally turn their luck around made them easy to fleece. Those kinds of hotels were easier to get comps at if she played the tables right. She just needed to build a roll respectable enough to make a run at Macao.

The dream.

Lisa stepped in from the dry heat of the night into the manufactured air of the hotel. She felt a strange mix of relief from the stifling temperatures and annoyance at the prickle of her skin. They kept the place cold enough to chill meat. Good for the saps, though, kept them awake and gambling instead of going to bed like they should. Some slot jockey shoveling coins into progressives with an 80% payout instead of playing the good machines. Some old sack of skin playing keno or pennies, just trying to draw out the time. They were paying for entertainment, not chasing the big score.

They were just as sad.

Lisa walked past them all. The floor was slow. She checked the board outside the poker pit and saw the best game was $5/$10. Not worth her time. She put her name in for $10/$20 and headed toward the elevators. She could use a shower to get the stink of that jackass Joe off her. The guy used too much body spray, and had leaned in as he talked, as if he had a chance. What a joke.

As she cleared the threshold into the elevator lobby, she paused. The oranges and reds that existed in a stream of regurgitation across the entire casino floor were gone, replaced by a soft green hue. She felt like Dorothy standing inside the Emerald City. The four elevators that had been there were gone too, replaced by a single elevator, old even by the hotel's standards. It looked like it should have a lift operator inside. Lisa's head blurred for a moment, and she thought she was drunk. It didn't matter how much she normally drank in a day. It didn't matter that it was over an hour ago that she'd left the bar without feeling much more than a buzz. In that moment, she was certain she was drunk. And with that feeling came the draw that she just needed to get inside the elevator before her.

But the door wasn't open.

Then the door opened.

Lisa swayed awkwardly for a moment before finally stepping into the elevator car. She turned and looked at the row of buttons. She had a twelfth-floor room, but the elevator only went up to floor nine. She stood there staring at the buttons as the elevator door closed. With a jerk, Lisa lost her balance and slammed against the wall, the impact shaking her from whatever haze she'd previously existed in.

"What the fuck?" she said in total confusion as she watched the arm of the floor dial rise to the third floor. The elevator jerked to a stop and the door opened, but Lisa didn't get out.

"This is your floor," said the small voice to her side. Lisa turned to look and saw a young girl, maybe ten years old, with blonde pigtails and purple bows in her hair. She wore an old dress, like some doll people tried to sell on those antique TV shows. "Are you getting off?"

"No," Lisa said. "This isn't my floor."

"I think it is," the girl said.

"How would you know?" Lisa asked, rubbing at her head, quickly figuring that she must have wandered into the wrong hotel. After a while they all started to look the same to her.

The girl held an ornate music box in her hands. "The Lift doesn't make mistakes."

Lisa didn't know what that meant, but she reached and pushed the button for the lobby. The elevator door didn't close. Lisa pushed the button again, feeling a sense of enclosure she didn't appreciate much with every rapid tap of her finger.

"That's not going to work," the girl said, her wide green eyes still staring at Lisa.

"How do you know?" Lisa asked.

The girl didn't answer, as if her silence itself was an answer.

"Whatever, I'll take the stairs," Lisa said, and took a step out of the elevator, into the hall. Immediately she heard the ding of the elevator door, and turned to see it closing behind her, too far away to reach. Somehow, Lisa was fifty feet from the elevator, and she reached out toward it as if to stop the inevitable. She glared at the little girl who stood in the middle of the elevator, blank-faced, as the doors closed.

Lisa stabbed her finger at the elevator button, but nothing happened. There was no movement, no sound, nothing. She spun and looked down the hall, looking for a sign pointing the way to the stairs, but again, nothing.

There had to be a way out. Even the old dump hotels had fire exits. Lisa began to walk. When the hall ended and split left and right, she chose right. When it ended again, she took another right. Circle or no, there had to be something. Except that after four rights, she still hadn't seen the elevator doors again.

Fucking casinos. They designed the gaming floors to be a maze to keep the saps in; they weren't supposed to make the room floors so damn complicated.

*Right.*
*Left.*
*Right.*
*Right.*
*Left.*
*Left.*

Nothing. Just the hallway and the doors. Doors with no numbers.

"Fuck!" she finally screamed, rubbing at her eyes with shaking hands. She slammed herself backward into the wall and let gravity do the rest, slumping to the floor.

The feeling almost hurt. Her eyes clenched shut, she gritted her teeth, her head cocked to the side. The memory in that moment roiled in her mind like a horrible whirlpool of hate and regret. She felt small again, sitting next to the closed door. The silent door.

The once silent door.

The muffled sounds of an argument on the other side slowly cleared like a dissipating fog.

"What am I supposed to think?" A woman's voice, full of spite and resentment.

A gulp of a drink. The slam of a glass on the counter. The grunt of air passing by lips on the pained burn of alcohol-fueled words. "You're supposed to be grateful that someone's showing her some fucking attention and she's not getting whored out on the corner."

The resounding smack of an open palm connecting to a face.

"Don't you dare talk like that to me," the woman said, her words a hiss of warning.

A moment of silence, then a chuckle. "You can take the girl out of the trailer park...fine...that's the way you want it. Be that way. I don't fucking need this."

Lisa withdrew deeper into herself, pulling her knees up to her chin and hugging them so tightly that the crooks of her arms hurt. Words, she could drown out. Then, the sound of a door opening. She sprang to her feet, ready to yell, plead, ask him to take her too...

But there was no one there. The hall was empty. All of the doors were closed.

Lisa's face twitched and she scratched at it, her fingers coming away wet. She was sweating, and crying.

"He wasn't your father, was he?" the posh little voice said.

Lisa's head snapped to the side, and she saw the girl again, standing just inside the open elevator doors.

"Shut up," Lisa said, stomping her way to the elevator and mashing the button for the lobby.

The girl clucked her tongue. "Being rude isn't going to help."

Lisa ignored her and looked between the buttons and the display over the door. The door closed, but the elevator didn't move. "What's wrong with this thing?"

"There's nothing wrong with it. You're exactly where you are supposed to be."

"What's that mean?" Lisa said, her voice cracking with the pressure of unwanted memories.

The girl didn't answer; she just stared back up at her. Lisa considered grabbing the ornate music box from her hands and smashing it on the ground, just so...just so...

"Just so you could make me feel what you feel?" the girl asked."If it would make you feel better..." The girl extended her arms, presenting the music box. Instinctively, Lisa snatched it from her hands with every intent to smash it, but the moment her hands touched the surface, it wasn't a music box anymore. It was a...

"Violin?" Lisa asked.

The girl looked at the violin, then back to Lisa. "I feel bad for you," she said.

"W-why?" Lisa asked. She could feel the tremble in her voice echo the shaking of her hands, holding the violin case, terrified to drop it.

The girl sighed. "Sometimes people see it as a cherished memory, something they hold onto, or even something they wished they could have kept forever. But for you...it's different. In a way."

Lisa stood outside of herself, in the rain, watching through a fogged diner window as a young girl, only eighteen years old, hungrily ate a meal, trying not to act hungry. Trying to act the part. The girl finished her meal and the waitress brought the check. The girl looked at total, then flashed a panicked glance around the booth. Nothing too big, but big enough. She flagged down the waitress, and her lips began to move.

Lisa didn't need to hear her; she knew the words. The pleas for forgiveness, that her purse was back in the hotel and she needed to get it. The glare in the career waitress's eyes as she listened to the girl already sized up as a deadbeat. But the girl was earnest, swore she would come back, even handed over her violin case as collateral, that it was the most important thing in the world to her, worth a thousand dollars.

Whether it was due to belief or sympathy or apathy made no difference; the girl was allowed to leave, to get her wallet and return.

Lisa stood, her hair and clothes soaked as the girl disappeared into the night. Maybe a minute later, as the waitress showed the violin to another server, a man walked up: a well-dressed, impeccably groomed man, who asked about the violin. An antiquities dealer who couldn't believe what they were holding. He offered them $5000 on the spot for the violin. The words were taken at first as a joke, but the man's convictions never faltered. Finally, the server said she couldn't. It wasn't hers to sell, but it was clear the words were hard to say. The man sighed in resignation, offering his card and asking for whoever the owner was to contact him immediately if they wanted to sell.

It didn't take long for the plans to come together. For the tips and spare cash to be pooled. No one questioned if the girl was coming back anymore; they just couldn't wait for her to return. When she did, cash in hand, the group of servers made her an offer on her violin. First $1000, their eyes almost shining green with deceit. She refused; it was special to her.

$1200? No.

$1500? A slow yes.

Cash was exchanged, and the girl left. The waitress who waited on her hardly noticed that she'd forgotten to close out the tab. Not that it mattered; they were looking at a $3500 profit. She couldn't wait for her shift to end...

The man in the nice suit, a suit he'd stolen off a luggage cart a month earlier, stood under the awning, away from the pouring rain. Lisa walked up to him and saw the smile on his face. Her own face beamed in return. She'd done well. He handed her two hundred bucks, her cut. As he explained, more than she'd need, anyway. He took care of her. They were a team. Even when things were bad and he'd yell and sometimes smack her, they were a team.

"What do you call it?" the little English girl asked.

Lisa's lips moved without thinking. "The Fiddle Game."

"Bit on the nose, don't you think?" the girl asked.

"Mike loved the classics," Lisa said, a pained smile tracing her face.

The girl shook her head again, reaching out and taking back the violin...no, the music box. "You'll have to excuse me, but I really don't understand all the terms you use for these things. Glim-dropper, Beijing

Tea, that one you did with the boy in the store, what was that one? Change raising?"

Lisa smiled more openly. "Force of habit. He was weak. Just a little bit of fun."

"More's the pity."

Lisa rubbed at her neck and let out a defeated sigh. "What do you want?"

The girl looked confused. "Pardon me?"

"Don't fuck with me, kid. I know a con when I see one. What's your angle? What do you want? I take something from your dad? Maybe split up some weak marriage that wasn't going to survive anyway? What do you want?" It was subtle, but Lisa felt a slight bump in the elevator, as if it were starting to move but thought better of it.

"What I want is of no consequence. My name is Victoria. I live here."

Lisa chuckled softly. "So what? Parents lost their house, or you went with the one who got kicked out?"

"It's a bit more complicated than all that," Victoria said. "But I honestly don't know you, and I don't want anything from you."

"Yeah, but you do want something, don't you?" Lisa said with a wry smile, catching the girl's words as they slid so coyly from her lips. She had promise.

Victoria shrugged and looked down at her music box. "Can I tell you a secret?"

"That wouldn't make it a very good secret," Lisa said.

Victoria nodded. "I suppose not, but it might help."

"Fine. If it gets me out of this little game, I'll bite."

"I always want the same thing. I want you to make the right choice. And I'm *very* sorry that you find yourself having to make a choice at all. As much as I enjoy the company, it makes me sad when people get on this lift."

Lisa shook her head in frustration. "How's that supposed to help me? How is that even a secret? You're just babbling. Stop being–"

"Such a baby?" Victoria said, finishing her sentence.

It was a guess. It had to be a guess. Sure, the saying was common enough, but the words cut, and Lisa felt the cool wave of prickles wash over her skin. The memories actually made her shiver. Lisa's vision began to blur as she forced herself to hold back the tears. "What choice?" she asked.

As if on command, the doors opened again. They were still on the third floor.

"Your choice is one of attrition," Victoria said, the word sounding too big and sophisticated for her posh little voice. "In a life filled with difficult moments, this will be the most difficult. Because you will live them all at once."

Lisa didn't understand, but she stood there, listening. Her legs felt weak. She wanted to sit down.

"In your life, you've complicated the lives of hundreds of people. Your games acted as turning points in many lives. I daresay that what you've made of your life may have been one of the most influential I've ever seen. You've touched so many lives with your lies. The man from earlier today: he carried with him a seed of doubt and distrust. At his most vulnerable, he didn't know if he could be close to another person. You cemented that thought. He'll die alone. The boy in the store, he didn't really want to quit his job. He said that sort of thing all the time, but they were just words. His register will come up short, and losing his job before he can find the sunlight will force him further into the darkness. Need I go on? A dollar here, a dollar there, it all mattered to someone when it left their pocket and went into yours."

Lisa stared at the little girl, angry at the words that seemed to mean so little to her. "You don't know what you're talking about. I didn't do anything to them they didn't let happen. *They* were greedy, *they* were horny, *they* were stupid. If it wasn't from me, it would have been from someone else."

Victoria shrugged again. "Maybe, but that wasn't what happened. *You* happened. But you can still be saved. If you want to be."

"Who said I wanted to be saved?" Lisa asked, pulling herself away from the sadness and building her walls again.

"You're here, aren't you?" Victoria asked. "Some part of you does."

Lisa looked down the hall for a long while before looking back at the little girl and her music box. "Fine, I'll play along. Let's say for just a moment that I went along with your little scam. What would I even need to do?" All Lisa wanted to do was leave. It wasn't the most she'd ever wanted something, not even close, but some things couldn't be compared.

"Go to the door, turn the knob, go inside," Victoria said, as if it were the most obvious thing in the world.

"Which door?" Lisa asked.

"It doesn't matter. You're inside all these doors. As I said, you've touched a lot of people."

"And then what?" Lisa said.

Victoria looked down at her music box. "That's up to you. It all depends on what you really want." She paused. "And how much you want it..."

"I just want to leave," Lisa said. Still, a part of her wanted to know what the con was. It had to be a con. Some random girl wasn't just going to offer her salvation, whatever the hell that was. Maybe it was a con worth learning. "Fine, fine...I'll do it."

She expected to see some glint in Victoria's eyes, some semblance of victory for getting her to say yes to the con, but there was nothing. If anything, she looked sad.

Lisa took a step off the elevator and looked back. "You coming?"

Victoria shook her head.

"What? You don't want to see how this plays out?" Lisa said with a mock laugh.

Those sad eyes kept staring. "I can already see how it will play out."

The elevator door closed, and Lisa watched the lights over the doorway move down. She sighed and turned, part of her wondering if it wasn't some kind of police sting to entrap her, another part not even caring.

So many doors to choose from. Lisa stopped randomly in front of one. It was as good as any other.

"Okay," Lisa said, "let's play…"

She reached forward and turned the knob.

One day, though not yet, she would spend her days wondering what would have happened, had she found the will to go into the second room.

The Fourth Story: Greed / Desire / Lust

# Cake
## by Nelson W. Pyles

### I

Julia looked at the text on her cell phone. She blinked a few times and read it again. Blunt and right to it.

*Mom's dead. When can you come home?*

Her brother was a lot of things, but subtle wasn't one of them.

She started to write several texts in response, mostly sarcastic, but decided to respond in kind.

*Tomorrow morning.*

She stared at the phone for nearly a full minute until the response came back.

*K*

She sighed.

She lived in Erie and was only about two hours from Pittsburgh, but it already felt like a million miles away. She slumped in her chair and stared at the picture on her office wall. It was her, her brother Vince, and her mom.

Her now dead mom.

She was going to text him back and ask what had happened, but she could probably guess. Too much booze, not enough insulin, drugs and so much more. She really didn't want to know. She had been done with her mother for a while now, and honestly couldn't care less.

What she did care about was the couple of days she was going to lose having to deal with funeral arrangements, her family, and her fucking brother.

She sighed again.

"Death is never convenient," an old girlfriend had told her once. "If it was, wouldn't you pick a better time than 'out of nowhere?'"

Julia smiled slightly to think of her: Marcie. "The Keeper," Julia had called her, until Marcie decided to be "the one that got away."

She looked hard at the picture. It had to be at least twenty years old. Her brother, three years younger, just barely a toddler and Julia, a surly-looking five. Their mother was in her early thirties, still beautiful, still present.

Before the divorce. Before it got really bad.

*No*, Julia corrected her line of thought. It was always bad. It was before Mom got stupid.

She looked down at her phone. She was going to have to ask how their mom died, but that could wait until seeing Vince. Julia picked up the phone. There was some work to do before driving to Erie, and there was no need to wait.

First, she had to cancel her appointments for the week, save for one: to look at a prospective purchase of some abandoned building that was, oddly enough, in

Pittsburgh. Julia wanted that one in process for buying soon, and wanted to get a closer look at the inside.

The sooner it was hers, the sooner it could get torn down. The sooner she could do what she did best.

The other appointments would still come through. In fact, the delay due to her mother's sudden death would probably add what Julia called the "sympathy bonus." Real estate folks sometimes kicked in a bit extra if there was a delay for deeply personal reasons. Your mom dying was a big one. Not so much grandparents, but parents, siblings, even kids. That was an easy ten percent overage on whatever she would stand to make.

It would help if she could learn to cry on demand.

This thought made her smile a little, and then she stopped herself.

*Am I that cold?* she thought. *Is it all just about money now?*

Somewhere inside of her, something nodded, and a little voice said simply, "Yes."

She nodded to herself and began to cancel appointments.

## 2

Julia stood at her mom's front door in Shadyside and hesitated to knock. There was an oddly overwhelming sense that she should just turn around and go back home. There wasn't anything for her here anymore. She looked at the mailbox. It was the shitty one she and Vince had made their mom one year for Mother's Day. What was she, twelve? Jesus, that was a million years ago.

It was an ugly wooden thing that their mom had immediately put up, replacing the old black one that hung off to the left of the front door. This ugly thing hung there now, like a cyst; all black and yellow, with the last name emblazoned in yellow paint, declaring METERUCCI. After the divorce, her mom had kept the name, refusing to go back to being the less exciting-sounding SMITH from her maiden years.

"Smith is boring," she'd said. "Meterucci sounds like you might be, you know…dangerous or connected, you know?"

Julia fought and won against the smile that almost spread across her face.

She knocked twice, hard, on the door.

After a moment, the door swung open. Vince stood there, hair screwed up, in dirty t-shirt and boxer shorts. He looked at her and sighed.

"You coulda just come in," he said, and walked away from the door, adding, "Come get some coffee."

She grabbed the door handle roughly and yanked it open. She walked in and, out of an old habit, dropped her keys in the large ashtray that sat off to the left on a small table. She regarded the old muscle memory with a grunt and walked through the living room into the small kitchen.

Vince leaned against the kitchen counter with two cups of coffee. He held one out for his sister, who took it. "Cream in the fridge," he said. "Sugar where it always is."

She said nothing and took a sip. She grimaced. "Instant?"

He smiled.

"I thought it was appropriate," he said, holding his mug out. Julia grunted and tapped his mug.

They both took a sip and made the same face.

"I never understood how she could drink this crap," she said.

Vince chuckled. "She was high all the time," he said. "She probably couldn't even taste it."

"True," she sighed. "So what happened?"

Vince laughed. "You waited until you got here to ask."

Julia frowned. "So what?"

"Just typical."

"Your text said 'Mom's dead.'"

"But you didn't *ask*."

"And you didn't *tell*. Spill it."

"How do you *think* she died?" he said, suddenly angry. "She was drunk and high. She fell and died on her back, choked on her own puke. Like a rock star. Like we *always knew* she was gonna die."

Julia joined his anger. "And you couldn't just *say* that, could you? Just had to half-ass it like everything else in your life. A 'Mom's dead' text. Beautiful, Vin."

He was going to say something else, but stopped.

"Look, I'm sorry," he said finally. "I was the one who found her. It was really messed up to see. I didn't know what to say. Never had to tell anyone someone was dead."

Julia looked at him, and his eyes were wet, but not exactly crying.

"Sorry," she said. "I didn't even think of that."

They just looked at each other for a long moment.

"This is so messed up," Vince said.

"Yeah," Julia said. "What do we do now?"

"Well," he started, "we have to pick out something for her to wear in the coffin at the wake."

"There's going to be a wake?" she asked. "Who the hell's going to go to that?"

"Us, for one thing."

"She didn't have any friends."

"How the hell do you know?" Vince snapped. "You haven't exactly been around. Or called. Or anything."

"There's a reason for that," she said. "And you damn well know it."

"What, cos she didn't approve of your little lifestyle? So what?"

"It's not my 'little lifestyle,'" Julia said. "I'm a lesbian. It's what I am, it's who I am. I didn't feel like hearing how I was going to hell every time I talked to her."

"That's just how she was," he said.

"Too bad, cos this is just how I am," she said back.

"You don't even see the irony in that, do you?"

"Oh, I do," she said. "It's just that my 'little lifestyle' isn't going to make me choke on my own puke."

They stood quiet again.

"We used to be close," Vince said quietly.

"We did."

"Why are we angry at each other?"

"I don't know that I'm angry at you."

He laughed. "Yeah, a little bit."

"You angry at me?"

He nodded.

"Why?"

"Because you left."

Julia shook her head. "No, that's not true. You *stayed*. Big difference."

"Somebody had to take care of her."

"Wrong. She needed to take care of *herself*. You needed to get out."

Vince looked at her hard. This time, he was crying. "But…it was *Mom*."

Julia drank the rest of her coffee in one disgusting gulp. "*Your* mom, certainly not mine," she said, and put the mug on the counter, hard. "I have to go check out a property. I'll be back in a few hours. We can discuss details later."

"A property? You're *working*?" His face was one of slight revulsion.

"That's right," she said. "I was going to be here eventually anyway. Might as well make the most of it. You'll be here, yeah?"

"Yeah," Vince said, turning away. "Of course. I'll be here. Always here."

"Right," she said, and left the kitchen.

## 3

Julia walked up to the old nine-story building. It was a little run-down looking, but with some work, she could turn it around, maybe into a really nice, hip apartment complex. It was super close to downtown Pittsburgh, and transportation was right out in front.

But it looked odd, somehow. Like it was brooding.

Or waiting.

She fought off a chill and walked to the door.

She didn't have a key, but sometimes these old buildings were open. If it was open, she could look around a bit. Not too much; an open door often meant squatters. She had pepper spray and a black belt. She wasn't too worried.

She couldn't believe Vince. How dare he talk to her like that?

*It was Mom.*

He just didn't get it. And saying it was her 'little lifestyle." Bastard. He'd never had to fight for anything, much less work for anything. She was a woman, and a gay woman no less.

She was also goddamn successful.

Not just a successful woman, but a successful *gay* woman.

All obstacles, and she beat them down. Screw anyone who couldn't respect that.

"Aren't you worried about hell?" Mom would say. "Don't you know it's evil?"

Then Julia would yell about how she just didn't understand.

"Aren't *you* worried about an overdose?" she'd yell back. "What hell is there for dead junkies, Mom?"

Every time.

The worst part was, her mother would tell her that she wasn't homophobic. She was just worried, but Julia didn't buy it. She'd say, "I love you, Jules, but I wish you'd just stop being gay."

Like it was a switch.

Julia was getting angry again. She was always angry anymore.

But happy content people didn't make money. And Julia Meterrucci made money.

She found the anger she always harbored was less when she closed a deal, or had a windfall of cash from a longshot paid off in dividends. Like her mom with drugs, Julia got high, but on cold hard cash.

She looked at the front door again and thought she could almost hear the money calling out to her.

She put her hand on the nice ornate doorknob and turned it slowly. She gave a small push, and it opened.

*Well*, she thought. *Here we go.*

Time to get high.

# 4

The entranceway was dark, as was everywhere she could see. A long hallway was in front of her, but that was really all she could make out. She took her cell phone out of her back pocket and found the flashlight app. She tapped it on and held it in front of her. It spat out bright light, but the hallway darkness seemed to eat it, making visibility limited. *Still*, she thought, *not going to fall over anything.*

Or anyone.

She walked slowly forward, moving the light onto things she wanted to see; some old framed paintings, some really nice fixtures, and a carpet that should have looked much more worn than what it looked like now.

There were no cobwebs. It looked almost cared for, although it had been abandoned for decades, perhaps longer. She continued down the hallway and stopped when she heard something like a chime. She held the light to the sound, and saw a little girl with something in her hands.

Julia dropped the cell phone and of course, the light went out.

"Oh shit," she said through her teeth. She dropped to the floor and felt around, looking for the phone. She didn't find it, and she began to panic a little.

"I've got it," said the little girl. "Don't worry, you're okay."

This did nothing to calm Julia down, nor did the fact that the voice was right in front of her. She looked up and saw the faint outline of the girl.

"Here you are," said the girl, holding out the phone. The girl's voice had what she thought was an English accent.

Julia slowly reached out and took the phone. She tried to get the flashlight back on, but couldn't.

"Damn," she said, shuddering.

"Don't worry," the little girl said. "I can provide some light."

The lights in the fixtures all began to glow and illuminate the hallway. It was still dark, but she didn't need the flashlight. It did nothing to soothe her.

"Why are you in here?" Julia said, a little rougher than she had intended.

"Where else should I be?" the girl replied.

"I don't know," Julia said. "Home?"

"My name is Victoria," the girl said. "Would you like a look around?"

Julia got back to her feet and looked at the girl. "Um…sure. I guess."

"Come this way," Victoria said, and turned. She walked down the hall and then stopped. Her head spun back. "Are you coming, Julia?"

"Yes, I'm coming," she replied, and walked after her. "How do you know my name?"

"I know the names of all my guests," came the reply. "It's only polite."

Julia had no response. She was still in shock about the lights coming up, and the little girl.

Victoria stopped at an elevator and pushed the button. "We're going up," she said.

"Oh, I don't think that works, honey," Julia said.

Just then, the green UP arrow lighted, and she heard the elevator arrive. There was the ding of a bell, and the doors opened.

"You were saying?" Victoria said, giggling.

"I don't think that's safe," Julia said flatly, not quite understanding what was happening.

"You've never been safer," Victoria said. "Let's see what floor we're going to."

Victoria walked into the elevator, but Julia hesitated.

"What is it?" Victoria asked.

"I'm afraid," Julia said without thinking.

Victoria smiled. "I know," she said. "That's why you're going to get on my lift. You've always been afraid."

This made absolutely no sense to Julia, but somehow that fact didn't matter.

It was true.

"Come along then, Julia. There are things to see."

Julia stepped into the lift, and the doors closed immediately behind her.

"So, what floor shall we go to?" Victoria asked.

"I have no idea," Julia said.

"I wasn't talking to you," Victoria said, and then the button that read *four* lit up.

Julia held her breath as the lift began to move. "What's happening?"

"We're going to the fourth floor, silly. Can't you see the number?"

"I can see the number, but I don't understand any of this."

"True, but that's never the point, is it? What's important is you will understand. Do you like music boxes?"

"Wait, what?"

"Don't get cross, it's a simple question. I'm going to answer for you: yes, you do. Listen."

Victoria opened her music box, gave the key a turn, and a very familiar song began to play.

It was "Rainbow Connection" from the *Muppet Movie*. Her mother's favorite song.

"It's an awfully pretty song, isn't it?"

"Can you stop that?"

Victoria closed the box, stopping the music. "Do you not like it?"

"No, I don't," Julia said, but she was lying.

"Maybe I'll play it again later," Victoria said.

The lift stopped and the bell chimed again. The doors opened. Julia looked out, expecting to see another darkly-lit hallway.

She saw her mother's kitchen.

"How the hell…"

Against everything inside, which was screaming, she walked off of the lift and into the kitchen. Almost as soon as she did, she smelled it.

Cake.

Her mother was baking a cake.

But her mother was dead.

And yet she wasn't, because Julia saw her walk into the kitchen, cigarette dangling out of her mouth. She looked at Julia and smiled. "Doesn't it smell good, Jules?"

Julia nodded and looked down for Victoria.

She was gone.

Julia looked behind her, and the lift was gone too. She was in her mother's kitchen, all alone with a dead woman.

Her head snapped around and found a cloud of blueish smoke from her mother's cigarette in her face. She coughed a little and waved her hand. Her mother gave a raspy laugh.

"Oh, stop it, it's not gonna kill you," Mom said.

Julia's head was spinning; this was one hell of a hallucination. It was a dream, it had to be. It seemed all so real, but she knew it was a dream.

Right?

"I'm glad you're here," her mom said. "Come sit down. We need to talk."

She reached up and ran her hand along Julia's face gently. She looked up at Julia and smiled sadly, then left the kitchen.

Julia stood there for a moment.

*Just a dream*, she thought.

She followed her mother out of the kitchen.

## 5

Her mother sat next to a window in the dining room. She had her smoke and her awful coffee cup, filled with even more awful instant coffee.

"Sit down, Jules," her mother said. "I need to talk to you."

Julia found a seat farthest from her mother and sat. She looked at her mother blankly.

"I know what you're thinking," Mother started. "I'm supposed to be dead. And I am."

"This is just a really fucked-up dream," Julia said.

"Sure," her mother said, smiling. "Then you're in a consequence-free environment. Nothing to fear. No need to hold back, right?"

"I guess..."

"You're a very angry woman," Mother said. "Do you think it's because you're a dyke? I've never really seen *happy* dykes."

This brutal sentiment snapped Julia back a bit from her daze. "That's a really lousy thing to say. You just called me *dyke*."

"That's what you are, isn't it?" Mother asked. "Is that not the right word? We didn't have them when I was growing up."

"That's bullshit," Julia said, getting louder.

"I wanted grandkids," Mother said. "Vince is never gonna have any. All I wanted was that, really. And for you two to be happy."

"You know you always said that," Julia said. "But all you really wanted was to get high."

Mother nodded.

"There was that," she said, "and look where that finally got me. But how could I *not* get high? Look at all I had to deal with."

"Oh, that's right, you're a victim," Julia said, laughing. "Gay daughter, lazy son, divorced, alcoholic drug addict. Certainly nothing you could have done wrong...except you've *always* been an addict."

"Well," Mother said with an air of indignity. "Not anymore."

"Why, because you're dead? That's a shitty way to kick drugs," Julia snapped.

"True, but it works," her mother replied, and gave a raspy laugh. "I've been clean for a whole day! Aren't you *proud?*"

Julia was almost too furious to notice how absurd this all was, and how unlikely. Part of her registered that this was an impossible conversation, but a much angrier part of her didn't care.

"I see you're angry," Mother said. "I don't blame you. My death has ruined your routine. How unfortunate. I truly am sorry. But I needed to talk to you."

"So you waited until you were dead," Julia said through her teeth. "Your timing sucks as it always sucked."

"Ooh, I have to check on the cake. Come give me a hand," Mother said suddenly. She got up and rushed into the kitchen.

Julia sighed and got up to follow her.

She walked into the kitchen and watched as her mother pulled the flattish-looking cake out of the oven. She inhaled; it certainly smelled like cake, but it looked like a flat pile of something, the way her mother's cakes always looked.

"I just don't know why they always look like this," Mother said as she put the cake on the counter to cool. "I follow the directions to the letter."

Julia laughed. "No you don't," she said. "Does that look like you followed the directions?"

Her mother frowned. "You used to love making cakes with me. And you always ate them."

"Well, they always tasted good, but you always left out eggs."

Her mother looked at her, somewhat shocked. "Eggs?"

"Always, eggs. Every single time."

"Well, when were you going to tell me?" Mother asked. "I mean, I'm dead now, so what good is it?"

Julia let out a snort. "I always told you. Every single time. You never listened."

"But you always ate it."

"I didn't want you to feel bad," Julia said quietly.

Her mother sighed. "So you just ate shit cake to spare my feelings?"

"Pretty much. Me and Vince. You seemed to enjoy making it and really, it was the only time you seemed happy. Why would I ruin that?"

Julia's mother pushed past her to go back into the dining room. Julia followed.

"What?" Julia asked. "Why, of all things, is that the one you feel bad about?"

Her mother sat down hard. She looked up at Julia, eyes welling with tears.

"You did try to tell me, didn't you?" She slammed a fist on the table. "Why didn't I listen?"

"Because you were high and drunk most of the time, Mom. You never listened to us. You never listened to me unless I told you something you couldn't handle. Apparently, putting goddamn eggs in a cake was one of them."

"You watch your mouth. Don't talk to me like that," Mother said.

"No," Julia said, sitting back down across from her. "I *will* talk to you like this. I'm an adult. I'm a successful adult. I *own* things. I'm rich, and I did it all responsibly. I don't get high, I don't not follow directions, and I've made something of myself. I did something, and I'm rewarded well for it, in spite of how I was or wasn't raised by you. All you did was tell me I was going to rot in hell for being a lesbian, but I actually *did* something with my life."

"I didn't want you to be alone like me," Mother said. "I never wanted you to suffer like me, or want for things you couldn't have because of what you are."

"What I am," Julia started, "is a goddamn *success* story."

"You're not a mother. You can't judge me. You and your brother didn't come with instructions."

Julia gave a harsh laugh. "That's what you always said. 'You kids didn't come with an instruction manual.' You didn't come with one either. And Jesus, you were just awful."

"Why didn't you ever say anything to me?"

"Because you're my mother!" Julia yelled. "*You* were supposed to be the responsible one. *You* were supposed to take care of *us*. You were supposed to take care of *me*. And what happened? Vin and I had to peel you off the floor in the morning. We had to clean you up so you could go to work, when you had a job. Instead of sleepovers and hanging out with the friends we could cobble together, we had to make sure you didn't choke on your own puke when you passed out. We raised ourselves. And frankly, Vince did a lousy job, but he still stayed and took care of you. He paused his whole life to keep taking care of you."

"But you just left," Mother said. "You didn't take him along. He just stayed here."

"That's not my fault," Julia said. "None of this is my fault. You messed up your life, and if I hadn't left, you would've messed up my life too."

"But haven't you messed your life up on your own?" her mother asked, crying. "No spouse, no children. Just you."

"I'm rich," Julia said.

"So?"

"What do you mean 'so'?"

"You don't have any family. You don't have any friends. You have your job and you make money. That's your whole thing, isn't it? Money. Are you even still a dyke if you're not with anyone? You have things, but what do you have? You don't give a shit about your brother, and you sure don't give a shit about me. You have money, but what do you actually *have*?"

"You don't get it, Mom. You never got it."

"No, you're wrong. I think finally I do get it. I was a shit mother. Still am, apparently. Honestly, I was never a good mother. I know that now." There was a hitch to her voice. "No. I've always known that. Awful mother, and I can't apologize enough for it. I don't think I *should* apologize for it, because it wouldn't mean anything. I love you and your brother. I always did, but I didn't love myself, because I don't think I should have ever been a mother."

Julia couldn't believe her ears.

"But I was a mother. I was just a really shitty one."

Julia felt a hitch in her throat gathering, but she cleared her throat. "Is this your idea of an apology?"

Her mother shook her head.

"No, not an apology. You wouldn't accept one if I gave it, because even though I admit I was a bad mom, I don't think I did anything wrong. I know I did, but it's much too late for that now. All I can do now is tell you what you already knew, and one more thing before you go."

Julia had been so wrapped up in what was happening, she'd forgotten that this shouldn't be happening at all. She had no idea how she was going to get back to wherever the hell she came from. And where was that little girl?

101

"And what's that?" Julia asked.

"Don't end up like me."

"Impossible," Julia said. "I'm nothing like you."

"But you *are*," Mother said. "You're filling a large hole that I carved into you because I was constantly trying to feel anything at all. Booze, drugs...nothing I should have been doing with two kids. But I couldn't feel anything except a total failure. You, you fill up on *things*. Money, property, stuff, and it feels good until it doesn't, and you have to do it again. And again. Sure, you're rich. But when you die..."

Her Mother pointed around the room.

"This is where I died. This is where I am now. This is what I built. Vince wants to have a wake for me, and you rightfully asked who was going to come to it. No one, that's who. You and him, and you don't have a single reason to, other than I'm your mother. I earned that. That's what I made. That's how I go out. A burden in life and in death."

Julia sat and looked at her mother. There was an expression on her face Julia had never seen before.

Acknowledgment.

"So don't you end up like me. You hear? I don't care that you're a lesbian. I never did, I'm just an asshole. I'm glad you have money, but don't try to fill yourself with anything that isn't good. You can't fill yourself with emptiness. You have people around you already that love you. Don't shut them out, even if it's just your brother. He needs you."

"So you die and suddenly you're fine that I'm gay?"

Her mother laughed.

"It's your life, Jules. It was something that made you happy, and I didn't get that. I still don't exactly get it, but it's part of you. Just like I'm always going to be part of you, and that's why you need to stop and hear me. Don't wind up like me. Be happy."

Julia simply stared at this woman, whom she had hated for most of her life. For a moment, she hated her even more than ever.

Her mother smiled. "I know," she said. "I'm infuriating. I always have been, but that's done now. I'm not going to see you after this. But I wanted to tell you this before you left. I love you, Julia."

Julia began to cry bitter and hard tears. She looked at her mother through them and found she couldn't speak.

Her mother stood up and went over to Julia. As Julia stood up, her mother grabbed her, hugging her hard. The cries from Julia came in loud wails and still, her mother held her.

"Shhhh, baby. Let it out," her mother said. "I'm so sorry, Julia. I'm so very sorry."

Julia hugged her mother back, just as hard. They stood that way for what felt like a long time. A time, Julia knew, that had to be coming to an end.

Her mother loosened her hold on Julia and looked at her. "I never saw you cry," she said.

Julia laughed a little. "I never had a reason to."

Her mother wiped her tears with her fingers. "You always had a reason to," she said, and kissed her daughter on the cheek. "How about some terrible cake?"

Julia and her mother laughed.

"Sit down, Mom. I'll go get it."

She started to turn to return to the kitchen, but her mother gently grabbed her and gave her another kiss.

"I'll be right back," Julia said, and walked into the kitchen. As she walked to the cake, still sitting there on the counter, she heard a bell chime.

It was the same chime from the lift.

She looked next to the cake, and there the lift was, open and waiting. Victoria was in there too, with her music box.

"It's time to go, Julia," Victoria said.

"But...we were going to have cake."

From behind her in the living room, she heard the opening banjo chords to "Rainbow Connection" playing on an old record player.

"I know," Victoria said sadly. "But we have to go now."

Julia stood there for a moment, listening to the song.

There were a lot of things she wanted to say to her mother. There were still things that were going to make her angry. She knew she could possibly never forgive her mother for some things, but for the moment, everything had already been expressed. Unspoken, in a really good hug and a cry.

Julia walked into the lift, and the door slowly closed behind her.

# 6

The lift reached the lobby, and the doors opened. The hallway was still lit from the old fixtures and she walked into it, followed by the little girl.

Julia just stood there for a moment, not really wanting to walk anywhere. She looked down at the little girl, whose eyes had a slight green glow to them.

"What *was* that?" Julia asked.

"It was a long overdue visit with your mum," Victoria said. "How do you feel?"

"I'm not really sure," Julia said. Her eyes were still wet with tears. "I wish I could've listened to that song with her one more time."

Victoria smiled. "Would you like to hear it now?" she asked. "It's still ready for you to listen to it on my music box."

Julia smiled. "Thank you Victoria, but I'm going to go back to see my brother. My mom had that song on a record player. It's still there, I think. I think we should listen to it together. We have funeral arrangements to make."

"That's probably a good idea," Victoria said. She reached out and took Julia's hand. "I'll walk you out, Julia."

Julia nodded.

The two of them walked in silence towards the front door. As they walked, the light fixtures began to dim. The sunlight streamed through the front door, lighting the way.

"I'm not going to buy your building," Julia said. "At least, I don't think I should."

"Well, that's a relief," Victoria said, chuckling. "Wherever would I go if you did?"

"Exactly," Julia said, chuckling herself. "Where else *should* you be?"

The two reached the door.

"I'll leave you to it, then," Victoria said.

Julia looked at Victoria and smiled. She bent down and gave the little girl a kiss on her cheek.

Victoria smiled. "Good luck with everything. Thanks for the visit, and the kiss."

She turned and walked into the darkness.

Julia watched until she couldn't see the little girl, or the glow from her eyes.

She smiled again.

She turned and walked into the light.

The Fifth Story: Self-Obsession / Narcissism

# Buying America
## by Daniel Foytik

The council hall was silent, aside from the shuffling noises as the council members flipped through their notes and prepared to vote.

John Gate took a sip from the now-warm glass of water on the table in front of him and waited patiently for the verdict. Normally the council wouldn't have been involved in a private sale like this, but since the old hardware store shared a common wall with the town library, the bylaws required approval.

"Will you fix that sign too?" Councilwoman Baxter asked.

"Yeah," Councilman Wallace added. "The flicker drives everyone crazy."

"Of course," John answered. "It can't be Great America Hardware if the 'Great' is broken."

The assembly chuckled at that, and John responded with a shrug and his best charming smile. But underneath the smile, he silently fumed. How dare they give him, John Gate, what was in essence a directive? He was *John Gate*, and they were lucky to have him here revitalizing Main Street. He did things the right way – *his* way. With everything he brought to this worn-out town, they should be asking what they could do for him.

Of course, the hardware store was just the beginning. He had big plans for this town.

"Any further questions?" Mayor Anderson asked the assembly.

Five heads shook.

"OK. Let's proceed with the vote, then."

It was very early in the morning at Great America Hardware. Inside, the store was dark, aside from the faint light of a small desk lamp and the soft glow from a computer screen. Outside, the letters R and E in "Great" flickered, buzzed, and finally went out. John had fixed the place up over the last few weeks, before this week's grand reopening: giving the store a good cleaning and a general facelift, painting the brick bright white, resealing the parking lot, and even adding a new awning above the front entrance. The worn-out, flickering sign, however, remained as it had been when he'd bought it from the retiring Joe Thomas. Because fuck them.

John looked up from entering the prior day's sales into his bookkeeping software and stared.

The girl was back for the fifth morning in a row.

This time she'd darted off into aisle number five, the one with assorted pipe fittings and other miscellaneous plumbing supplies. She wore a Victorian-style dress, with her hair done up in pigtails and bright purple ribbons, like something out of a school play, or one of those steampunk conventions.

He considered whether or not to get up and look. He clenched his right hand into a tight fist to stop it from quivering. Mornings weren't the only times she'd appeared, but those were the most disconcerting, since the store was empty aside from him. During the day, her appearances and disappearances could be shrugged off as her slipping out the front door or ducking behind a group of customers, but in the mornings, he knew there was no explanation. He was alone from 5:00 am until 6:30 am, when his staff knocked on the front door to be let in.

*It's not my imagination; I know I saw her.* But that just wasn't possible. The door was still locked - he could see it from here. Last night, he'd made *sure* the store was empty. He'd walked every aisle, checking the security camera app on his tablet, watching himself move from frame to frame, from camera to camera. No, this store was empty last night and empty when he came in this morning.

He pulled the cameras up on his computer screen and clicked on the live feed for aisle five until it filled the screen.

Empty.

*I know I saw her.* As if in response, the child stuck her head around the corner and waved, then ducked back behind the shelves with a giggle.

He looked at the monitor and was again presented with an empty aisle.

"Peek-a-boo, peek-a-boo, I see you!" the girl's voice echoed in the empty store.

This was new. She hadn't spoken before, and he really wished she hadn't now. The sound of her voice - clear and accented and with an odd distorted echo - made his mouth instantly dry.

He sat staring at the monitor, afraid to look back up to the spot where she'd poked her head around the corner. Her voice called out again, clear and determined and impossible to ignore. "Peek-a-boo, peek-a-boo, you bad, bad man. Time is nearly up – better change while you can."

The loud rap on the glass made him jump and pulled him back to reality. Had he nodded off? Had he been dreaming?

He looked up to see three of his staff waiting to be let in.

Gary Wilson pulled on his collar and twisted in his chair uncomfortably, unable to make eye contact with his boss. He tried to calm himself by counting the tiny scratches and imperfections on his boss's name plate as the sun glinted from its surface.

"Are you listening to me, Wilson?"

Gary jumped and mumbled his assent without looking up, still struggling to form words.

"I don't know what's so hard to understand here!" John bellowed at the young man. "When I bought the store from that old codger, I said things were going to change and I meant it! I'm here to bring life to this town, and the right kind of clientele to this store."

John clenched and unclenched his fists as he stared at Gary over his desk. "This town used to be something! When I was a boy and I lived here, there were morals! There was an understanding of what was right and what was wrong. We *never* would have tolerated two women acting like that out in the open. Never!

"I left New York and came back here because I was tired of that sort of thing. And now? Now I find that people just turn a blind eye to it!"

Gary felt anger welling up inside that helped push him through his stunned silence. "Judy and Sally have been shopping here for years, sir. And they fixed up that old house into one of the best bed and breakfasts in the county. Before they bought it, it was an eyesore. You, talking about revitalizing the town? That's just what they…"

"Don't sass me, son! I think you forget who you're talking to. I'm sure there are plenty of people in this town who'd be grateful to have your job."

Gary took a deep breath and closed his eyes. This job was getting more awful every day, but he needed it. He felt a twinge of anger at Mr. Thomas for selling it to Gate and moving to Arizona. Then he felt ashamed - Mr. Thomas was a good and kindly man, and he deserved a nice retirement. If he'd known this was how Gate was going to run the place, Gary was sure Thomas never would have sold to him.

"Are you still with me, Wilson?"

"Yes, sir. I understand, sir."

"I'm glad to hear it. Don't make me remind you again. If they come back, you send them to me. I'll explain Romans 1:26 to them. This is a privately-owned business. I don't have to serve deviants here."

\* \* \*

He didn't see her, but he heard her footsteps darting down the general hardware aisle.

John took a deep breath and reached for his coffee. He suddenly felt cold, and the warmth of the liquid inside might restore a little of what he'd lost.

The girl giggled as he took a sip from the Styrofoam cup.

"Peek-a-boo, peek-a-boo, you bad, bad man," called the girl's voice. He looked at the monitor, and this time he *could* see her - she was playing hopscotch on the black tiles of the aisle and staring right into the camera.

"I've been watching you, Mr. Gate. I know what you say and do, but still you ignore me and the warning I gave. Time is nearly up. "

The image on the screen flickered and winked out as the knocking on the glass came. John jolted back to reality. Surely, he'd nodded off this time. Coming in so early every morning was taking its toll.

Dream or no, he felt even more unsettled than yesterday as he stood up and made his way to the door, keys in hand.

\* \* \*

"Why do we want all these people from shithole parts of the county coming here?" Gate asked Bethany Mills, the girl in charge of his paint department.

"I...uh, I'm not sure what you mean, Mr. Gate," Bethany answered.

"I asked you to run the ad for this week's special deals, and you sent it out to not only the *Reynard Chronicle*, but to the *Washington County News*, and even the *North Yancy Times*. So I ask you again: why would we want all these people from the shithole parts of the county coming to our store?"

When Bethany sat in stunned silence for several seconds, Gate continued, as if explaining to a child. "If you run ads in the papers from the shithole towns, you get shithole people in here. That's something the respectable people don't appreciate."

"But we've always run ads in those papers. Mr. Thomas always said he ran ads in all the papers within 50 miles, so that..."

"I don't give a good goddamn what that daft old coot did! I'm not him!"

"Clearly," Bethany muttered.

"What did you say, girl? Are you trying to be flip with me?"

"No, sir," she replied. "I...I was agreeing with you. You're nothing like Mr. Thomas. I'm sorry I ran the ad in the other papers without checking with you."

Gate nodded. "Well then, that's better. And if anyone from those parts comes in wanting those offers, you send them to me. I'll tell them it's a misprint – fake news! You can't trust anything those two rags print anyway, and everyone knows it."

\* \* \*

It was still too early for the birds. The dark parking lot and equally dark store had an ominous feel this morning.

John stood before the store and dug for his keys with one hand, while he tried to balance the drink carrier holding two large coffees with his other. He managed to pull out the keys but lost his grip on the carrier, and it tumbled from his hand. The Styrofoam cups exploded as they hit the sidewalk and scalding hot coffee splashed up, showering his legs.

John pulled in a deep screaming breath and dropped the keys. He looked at the puddle of steaming coffee and watched as it slowly snaked its way across the concrete and trickled into the storm drain. He bent over and picked up the keys and looked at the locked door.

"OK. There are no creepy little girls in my store. There are *no* creepy little girls in my store."

He picked up the mess from the sidewalk, unlocked the door and stepped inside, locking the door behind him.

He stood for a moment: listening, waiting, feeling the space with some primal part of himself that humans try to ignore most of the time, and knew she was there. He couldn't see or hear her, but she *was* there – somewhere, on the other side of a shadow, or behind the tiny space of a dust mote, she waited to slip into his reality.

John flipped the lights on and whistled as he moved towards the counter where his computer waited. His whistling echoed back to him from the back wall of the empty store, but he was sure he heard another whistler joining him, matching him note for note. He stopped, and the other whistle did too. When he started up again, the other whistler joined in.

He did his best to ignore it, slamming his keys down loudly on the counter next to his PC and slipping into the chair in front of it.

John worked for about 20 minutes, the only sound the shuffle of paper and the clickety-clack of his fingers on the keyboard as he entered the figures from the prior day. He felt silly for letting himself get freaked out earlier and rubbed his eyes, resting his head in his palms for a moment.

*I'm so exhausted. The stress is starting to get to me.*

"Peek-a-boo, peek-a-boo, you bad, bad man," called the girl's voice.

John kept his face in his palms, refusing to look up. His mouth was dry and his palms were ice cold.

"You really aren't even trying, are you?" The girl sighed. "Unless you change, it's going to be a very bad time for you."

John breathed deeply, rapidly, but refused to look up.

He felt tiny cold hands grip his own and pull them quickly away from his face…

His forehead hit the countertop just as the knocking on the glass came. He jolted back to reality.

"Jesus, that felt too real," he said with a shudder as he rose to let in his staff.

\* \* \*

"No, there's *no way* we're paying that!" John yelled into the phone. "I don't care what the last owner did, we aren't doing it."

John pulled the handset away from his face and stared at it for a moment, as if he could look through the holes in the receiver and see the crazy person on the other end of the line. He brought the handset back to his head.

"That sounds like your fault! You promised the kid a scholarship because the last guy wanted to dump money into the summer arts program? You just assumed I'd continue a program like that? You know what happens when you assume, right?"

He slammed the handset down in its cradle.

A timid knock came from outside his office, and Riley Jackson peeked around the corner.

"What?!"

"I'm sorry, Mr. Gate, but I couldn't help overhear…You're cancelling the annual scholarship for the summer art program?"

"That's right. If these kids what to waste their time on doodling, writing, or whatever other artsy-fartsy thing they think is more important than learning how to be responsible, that's their business. I'm not

taking a dime out of my business to encourage that crap."

"But, sir, art is important! It's how we bring purpose and meaning to our lives. These kids rely on our support to pursue their summer projects."

"You're on thin ice, Jackson. No one questions me in my own store."

The phone rang and Gate answered it, waving his employee off. "And close the door."

John sat on the couch and unwrapped another greasy hamburger as he watched the evening news.

The news.

Even that was a joke. The weather girl was fat, the female anchor was a Mexican, and the other anchor...yeah, John knew what he was.

This town had really gone down the shitter. He almost regretted coming back. He remembered it as a different place than this: a town with old-fashioned values, where a man didn't have to be afraid to let a woman know he appreciated the cut of her blouse and the way her skirt fit just so. A town with morals, where the deviants knew better than to shove their unnatural choices in everyone's face. A town where the lower classes knew their place and stayed out of your way. A town where a man could go to the local bar for a few beers and wouldn't get called a bigot for making a goddamn joke. What the fuck had happened to this place?

The way things had changed made him angry.
Really angry.

He remembered green lawns and his mother cuddling him on the front porch, her pushing him on the swing all summer long. When he grew up in this town, summer meant Kool-Aid and lightning bugs in old mayonnaise jars; fall was trick-or-treat for full-sized candy bars, TP-ing old man Betterson's huge oak tree, and tic-tacking on Devil's Night; winter was snowball fights and caroling, and *everyone* wished each other Merry Christmas instead of Happy Holidays. Now traditions were gone, people didn't know their place, and even something as simple as *male* or *female* were forgotten concepts.

He fell asleep with a half-eaten burger on his chest, the news droning on, and a deep frown on his face.

The first thing John noticed was the ache in his back, and the vibration and shuddering sound. He opened his eyes to find himself slumped in the corner of a tired old elevator. One that probably *had* been fancy in its day, but that was obviously long, long ago.

The girl stood with her back to him, facing the panel. Her anachronous outfit looked straight out of the 19th century. Ancient. But every aspect of it – from her lavender dress to the floral pattern of her sleeves – seemed like it had just come out of a high-end shop only yesterday.

She turned her head slightly and looked at him out of the corner of her eye.

"Oh, good. You're awake. I thought you'd never wake up." She wrinkled her nose. "You smell."

John looked down at the large grease stain on his shirt and brushed at it with orange Cheetos-stained fingers, then looked up at the girl. Things weren't right here. Everything looked solid and real enough, but something about this place spoke to the deep, instinctual part of him that most people try to ignore. It said that this wasn't his reality, that he'd slipped a tiny fraction of a fraction from normal: out of his own world and into another. This was someplace...in between.

"Where am I?"

"Oh, you're going to love it, John. It's another place *just* for you." She giggled. "The other versions weren't quite right, obviously. I know how much you enjoy being the center of attention."

John had no idea what she was talking about. He groaned as he pulled himself to his feet. His right leg had gone numb from the way he'd been sitting. "Who are you? How did I get here?"

"Oh, you've forgotten," she said, turning. "I'm Victoria. I'll be your...guide today. As to the rest, I don't want to spoil the surprise," she said with a giggle. "Surprises are ever so much fun, aren't they?"

She turned back to face the door as the elevator continued to rise, its accent punctuated at regular intervals by the sounding of an old-fashioned elevator bell.

John's anger rose, and he forgot the surreal and rather paranormal elements surrounding him. He reached out to grab the little brat.

*I'll shake some sense into this kid. Sometimes a good smack or shake is just what a kid needs to show her that adults are to be respected.*

"I'd seriously advise against that, Donald."

John stayed his hand and tilted his head.

*Donald? Why did she call me that? And why does it feel somehow...familiar?*

The elevator slowed, and then stopped with a lurch. The bell rang, and the doors slid open.

"Here we are again. Fifth story."

*Again?*

John looked around. It was just an old hallway. But then again, it wasn't.

The carpet was threadbare and worn, and the silk was frayed and peeling from the walls. Old Edison wall sconces jutted out from the walls; most were burned out or broken, but enough still worked that he could see the many doors lining the hallway that went on far longer than seemed possible.

*There's something familiar about this place.*

"Come along, Donald." Victoria stepped out of the elevator and walked down the hallway.

"I'm John. John Gate. Why are you calling me Donald?"

"Ah yes, that's right. You *were* John the last few times. John Barron, John Miller, John Gate. You really like the name John. And of course there was that time

121

you were David Dennison, but I'd rather not talk about that."

These names. They meant something. But what? He couldn't remember. It felt like trying to remember the name of someone you'd met long ago – like at a party in college – many years afterwards.

*It's almost...almost like something from another lifetime.*

Victoria stopped and turned. She was about thirty feet away from him. John still lingered in the elevator.

"I've been here before," he said, half statement, half question.

"Yes, Donald, you've been here for quite a long time now. It really was the safest for...well, for *everyone*. I do keep hoping you'll learn, but the choice continues to be yours."

John stepped out of the elevator and winced. *His head throbbed, and he was suddenly sitting, surrounded by a group of people. They were all talking at once - accusing him - and he felt his temper rise. How dare they come after him!*

Just as suddenly, the scene was gone, and he was back in the dim hallway that smelled of dust and age, staring at the little girl in the purple dress.

"Jesus Christ," John said. "What the hell *was* that?"

"Did we have a little time slip, Donald?" she asked. "It's OK, you'll start to remember things now. It's the only way you'll learn. You need some perspective before we move on to the next scenario."

John took a few steps and stumbled.

*He was sitting with five men with thick Russian accents, going through a stack of papers. He felt nervous, but also elated. This would all be over soon, but it would be good for his brand regardless.*

Then, John was on his knees, back in the hallway again, and Victoria was standing over him, holding that oddly luminescent music box of hers.

He was surprised to find that he remembered this, remembered being in exactly this situation before.

He knew her. He remembered. He knew her *and* that music box.

*Jesus, I'm still here.*

She closed the box. It seemed to disappear somewhere into the folds of her dress, but John knew that wasn't exactly right.

She reached out her hand and he took it, surprised as always by the strength of the tiny child, as she pulled him to his feet. She looked concerned. No one had looked truly concerned for him in such a long time, yet somehow this girl was able to do it.

"You've been here a long time, Donald," she said gently. "It gets harder to keep it straight. I suggest you choose well this time. You'll begin to lose yourself soon.

"You'll become like them," she said, nodding over his shoulder. "The ones who can't remember themselves any longer."

John turned his head and looked down the hallway. He could almost see them, almost make them out. Shadows...the cast-off layers of other men and women, who'd become so lost in this place that they existed in a perpetual unreality.

John felt himself pulled along through the hallway by the girl.

They were moving faster now, toward a horizon of hallway that went on forever. He watched as the doors on either side flew by faster and faster as they ran down the endless corridor.

"Hurry, Donald," Victoria called, her voice seeming far away even though she was right in front of him. "There's less time than I thought."

She opened the next door and pushed him through it. "Choose well this time."

The girl was back again. John had learned a long time ago not to talk about the little girl in the purple dress with blonde pigtails. No one else saw her, but he did.

He stared at the television and watched the politician bluster and drone on about how he was going to fix things, how he was going to bring back the glory days. He attacked his opponent for being crooked and duplicitous, then managed to contradict himself half a dozen times in the next ten minutes of his speech. He just kept going. He looked overly confident and self-assured. He sounded like a racist and a bigot. He was cocky and dangerous.

"That's you," said the man next to him. "You may have a different face, but I see you. You can't fool me, Donald!"

John looked at him and shook his head. "I don't know what you're talking about, Jimmy."

Jimmy tittered and tugged on his beard. He petted his own left hand with his right, as if it was a small kitten. "Oh, you'd *like* to think that. You'd like to pretend that's not *you* up there, but you can't hide from the truth! I know why you're here. *She* put you here." He pointed to the little girl. "Just like she did to me. I see you, kid!"

John stood and walked away.

The girl walked alongside him as he made his way back to his room.

"Do you want to talk about it?" the girl asked.

John ignored her.

*That's the only way I'm ever going to get well. It's like Doctor Mann says – I need to ignore her until she goes away.*

The girl stopped at the doorway as John entered his room. She stood in the hall, watching him as he climbed into bed.

That was the easy part. Ignoring her.

The hard part was convincing himself that it wasn't him on the TV, and that he wasn't about to become the most powerful man in the world. He allowed himself a grin. When that happened, maybe he could switch places with himself and get back to where he once belonged.

The girl sighed and wound her music box, then walked off down the hallway, the sound of the melody fading as she got farther away. The last thing he heard before he drifted off to sleep was the sound of Jimmy yelling that he hated that song.

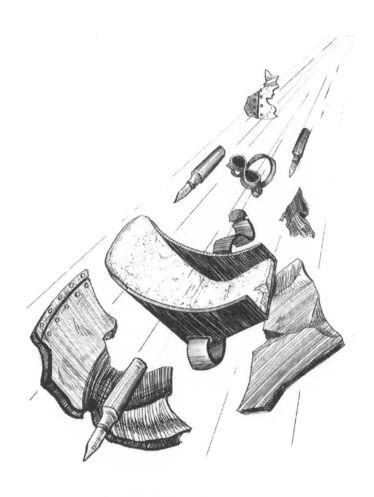

The Sixth Story: Denial / Grief

# The Final One
## by Charles Rakiecz

*DECEMBER 10, 2015*
*MERCY HOSPITAL*
*PITTSBURGH, PENNSYLVANIA*

Navy veteran Robert M. Scott listened to the monotonous *beep-beep-beep* of the heart monitor beside his hospital bed and sighed.

Scott had suffered a massive heart attack. One by one, his bodily functions were shutting down. He was dying and didn't have much time left. Still, he was at peace with that dreadful fact. After all, nobody could expect to live forever. Especially if, like Scott, they'd managed to reach the ripe old age of ninety-four.

Scott's family had been notified and were on their way to the hospital. That gave him a modicum of comfort. Even so, he was more concerned that a strange little English girl would arrive too late to see him off. She had assured him she'd be there at the end.

*What was her name?* he asked himself. *A queen's name. Yeah ... Victoria, that's right. How could I forget? Mind like a sieve.*

Although Scott's memory was spotty and his vision was gone, his hearing remained as sharp as ever. He overheard an orderly talking to a doctor in the hallway.

"Hey, Doctor Grant, what's this I hear about the old guy in 312-E being some kind of war hero? I know he was a pilot for United Airlines, but he's way too old to have flown jets in Desert Storm."

"Watch it, Dunnmire. First of all, that 'old guy' just happens to be *Mister Scott* to you – show some respect."

"Yeah, okay, sure, Doc. Sorry about that."

"Second, he was a WWII U.S. Navy torpedo bomber pilot during the Battle of Midway in the Pacific. Of eighty-four men in the three torpedo squadrons that attacked a superior Japanese carrier force, he was one of only fifteen who survived the battle. They say he –"

*"Doctor Grant – Doctor Grant – STAT – Extension 451."*

"I got to go. Do yourself a favor, Dunnmire, and look it up in a history book, or – oh, hell – just check the damned internet," Grant said as his voice faded down the hallway.

"Battle of Midway, huh," Dunnmire mumbled. "Maybe I'll order Charlton Heston's movie *Midway* on YouTube."

*What the hell did they teach Dunnmire in school?* Scott wondered. He groaned from a sharp stab of pain in his chest. He gasped for breath and gritted his teeth. *It … it sure wasn't American history or critical thinking.*

The elephant sitting on Scott's ribcage rose and left the room. His breathing eased.

*Dunnmire will probably skip the … movie credits, and never realize Universal hired my Navy flight school buddy George Gay, the only Torpedo-8 survivor, as a … a technical advisor for the film. Or that Kevin Dobson … played him on screen. Probably doesn't even … even know who Dobson is.*

A fresh wave of pain washed over Scott.

*I wish … Vic … Victoria would … show up.*

The heart monitor's beeping went wild.

The electronic sound faded away as Scott's life unreeled before his mind's eye. Not from the present and on back to the past, as he'd expected, but from the beginning.

*Newly born Robert M. Scott's behind slapped by the delivery doctor.*

*Little Bobby taking tentative first steps toward his mother's waiting arms.*

*Finger-painting in kindergarten.*

Scott's life rocketed past his conscious mind.

*Playing tag in the schoolyard during recess.*

*Riding a bike while delivering the morning edition on his newspaper route.*

Every detail was exactly as he remembered.

*Sweating through a high school Spanish test.*

*His first kiss.*

Each bittersweet memory threatened to overwhelm him.

*Dancing with his sweetheart at the senior prom.*

*Leaving home for the first time – college bound.*

*His days at Carnegie Tech cut short by the threat of war.*

*Enlisting in the Navy at a local post office.*

Scott detected a slight slowing in the passage of time.

*Navy boot camp and flight school.*

*His first solo flight in a Navy "Yellow Peril" N2S Kaydet biplane primary trainer.*

*Landing qualification flights on the Great Lakes paddle-wheel carrier USS Wolverine.*

The passage of his life really was slowing down.

*Training in a Douglas TBD-1 "Devastator" torpedo bomber.*

*Hearing radio newscasts of the Pearl Harbor attack, December 7, 1941.*

The slowing continued.

*Ensign Robert M. Scott reporting for duty aboard CV-5, the USS Yorktown at Pearl.*

Time ratcheted down and unfolded at normal speed.

*Torpedo Squadron Three … Torpedo-3 … VT-3 … Victor-Tango-Three …*

*0955 – 4 JUNE 1942*
*PACIFIC OCEAN,*
*WEST-NORTHWEST OF MIDWAY ATOLL*

Ensign Robert M. Scott's headphones crackled to life as his CO, Lt. Commander Lance E. "Lem" Massey, broke radio silence on the Tactical-4 channel : *"Victor-Tango-Three, Victor-Tango-Three … this is Lem-One … Tally … Jap fleet … bearing Two-Five-Niner … range fifteen miles."*

A sudden jolt of turbulence hit Scott's slow-moving Douglas Devastator. The plane bounced and shimmied side-to-side like a kite in a wind storm. The other twelve torpedo bombers in the squadron bucked and weaved like a drunken chorus line.

"You okay back there, Gunny?" Scott asked his young rear-seat gunner, Franklin S. Cole, over the Devastator's intercom.

"S-s-sure thing, Skipper," Cole replied with a nervous laugh. "Just like ridin' the … the Tilt-A-Whirl at C-C-Coney Island."

Commander Massey's voice came over Tac-4 again. *"VT-3 … descend for attack … angels Five-Zero. Good luck, men. Go in and hit 'em hard."*

Scott eased his joystick forward while checking his air/fuel mixture and rate of descent. "Here we go, Gunny. Hang on." His stomach fluttered like a first-time rollercoaster rider's.

Ugly black puffs of anti-aircraft fire dotted the sky ahead. Far below, ghostly-gray behemoths – Japanese aircraft carriers, battleships, cruisers and

132

destroyers – sliced curving white wakes into the sea. They were taking evasive action while under attack from a rag-tag assortment of Navy, Marine, and Army Air Force land-based units launched from Midway.

Few, if any, of the Japanese ships appeared to be damaged. Unfortunately, numerous flaming scythes cut through the azure skies above the enemy vessels. Scott realized those were the smoke trails of American planes shot down by the ship's guns, or the deadly Mitsubishi A6M Zero fighters.

"Skipper, you s-s-scared?" Cole asked.

"Damn straight. I'd be crazy if I wasn't."

"Good … good to know."

"Keep your eyes peeled for Jap fighters." Scott said.

"Roger that. Let's bag one of Tojo's carriers."

Skimming the waves at their 50-foot attack altitude, the planes of Torpedo-3 spread out and assumed a wide "scouting line" formation for the run-in to the massive enemy fleet. A smattering of ineffectual anti-aircraft fire came their way from the still-distant Japanese ships.

The flack lessened then stopped entirely.

Cole snickered. "Hey, Skipper, do you think the Japs ran out of ammo?" He answered his own question. "Holy shit! There's a huge flock of Zeros coming in fast behind us."

Cole opened fire with bursts from his single .30 caliber machine gun. The first pair of Zeros roared through the formation of lumbering Devastators like they were standing still. The Zeros' machine gun and 20mm cannon fire claimed one torpedo bomber. It trailed black smoke, banked to the right, and cartwheeled into the sea.

"The bastards just got Butler's plane." Cole fired as the next wave of enemy fighters closed in at over 300 miles an hour.

Straining to maintain an airspeed of 120, with a heavy Mark-13 torpedo slung from its belly, Scott's Devastator felt like an old plough horse trying to out run Seabiscuit in the Kentucky Derby.

Commander Massey's anxious radio voice called out for air cover from *Yorktown's* squadron of six F4F Wildcat fighters. *"Thatch from Lem One ... Thatch from Lem One ... answer."*

No reply.

They were on their own.

Like a hive of angry wasps, the A6M Zeros swarmed everywhere, dispensing death and destruction. They tore the American squadron to shreds on each pass, then looped around for another go at the outclassed Devastators.

Angry shouts and screams of pain erupted in Scott's headphones as other VT-3 planes succumbed to the relentless attacks. Scott glanced to his right and saw Commander Massey's plane trailing smoke as it flipped on its back, dove into the ocean, and exploded. Scott snapped his TBD hard left to avoid the debris-laden fireball. The maneuver saved his plane, but threw him out of formation for the torpedo run. The squadron was down to six planes, but only five were on target. Scott banked around in a full circle, trying to rejoin his squadron mates. He watched as the other VT-3 planes bore in on the enemy carrier, *Hiryu*, and dropped their torpedoes before most were shot down.

Unfortunately, the trouble-prone Mark-13 "fish" lived up to its poor reputation. Some torpedoes veered off to the left, out of control, while others ran too deep or "porpoised" through the wave tops. Of those running hot, straight, and normal, a few missed their fast-maneuvering targets, while those that hit failed to explode.

"Skipper, our torpedoes are crap," Cole said, mirroring Scott's own thoughts.

Scott cursed the Navy's Bureau of Ordnance weapon designers. So many American deaths – and to what end?

The Imperial Japanese Navy's four aircraft carriers, *Kaga, Akagi, Soryu,* and *Hiryu*, remained unscathed. They could easily destroy the smaller US fleet headed by the carriers *Hornet, Enterprise,* and the damaged *Yorktown*. Admiral Nimitz' battle plan, a desperate throw of the dice based on broken Japanese naval code intercepts, was about to come up "snake eyes."

An IJN destroyer steamed directly into the path of Scott's Devastator. He pressed his control stick button and the plane's lone forward-firing machine gun sent tracers streaming toward the enemy ship. It did little to suppress the hostile anti-aircraft fire.

Scott wished his plane had more guns – bigger guns – to fight with.

The Japanese gunners returned fire as Scott and Cole roared over them. All of the ships were firing at the tattered remnant of *Yorktown's* VT-3, as well as any survivors from *Enterprise's* VT-6 and *Hornet's* VT-8 torpedo squadrons attacking from other directions.

"My God, Skipper, I think they just about wiped out all three of our squadrons," Cole said in an anguished voice. "We might be the only ones left. Damn these piece-of-shit Douglas torpeckers."

Scott and Cole closed in on another carrier.

"We've got one last chance to make this right, Gunny. That looks like the *Kaga* up ahead."

The Japanese carrier's ack-ack batteries fired at Scott's plane while the vessel hard-turned to starboard to throw his aim off. Scott compensated by pulling out to the right and swinging back, giving him a perfect torpedo setup. Every gun on board the carrier seemed to be shooting at him now.

The torpedo dropped away, and the Devastator lurched upward from the sudden loss of dead weight. Scott pulled up and over the carrier's port side and did a flipper turn near the ship's island. He flew right down the centerline of the flight deck, safe, for a few seconds, from the murderous anti-aircraft fire.

"Holy shit, Skipper. I saw the Jap captain on the bridge walkway, jumping up and down, pointing at us and raising hell."

"Gunny, can you spot our torpedo's wake from back there?"

"Yeah, I think it's gonna ... it's gonna – Damn, it missed."

"Let's get the hell out of here."

Before they could climb and get away, a line of five Zeros dove down behind them. Bullets and 20mm cannon shells riddled the Devastator's tail and rear fuselage. Cole cried out in agony.

"Gunny, are you all right? Gunny – speak to me."

No reply. More 20mm shells blew holes in the wings.

As the third Zero made its pass, something exploded near Scott's left rudder pedal. Pain seared through his left leg and arm. His rudder control and aileron cables were shot out.

With blood puddling in his boot and running down his arm, Scott fought a losing battle to keep the plane level. The right wing hit a wave crest, and the plane pancaked into the ocean.

The impact snapped the plane around, slamming the "bird cage" canopy shut. The canopy resisted Scott's efforts to force it open.

"Gunny, we gotta get out now! GUNNY?"

Pounding on the canopy release, Scott realized they had failed. No, *he* had failed – his country, the Navy, his squadron, and Cole. Guilt and despair tore at him.

Salt water flooded the cockpit from every crack, seam, and bullet hole. It rose to Scott's waist –

his chest – his chin – his nose was under water. He was going down with the plane. His lungs were ready to burst.

Finally the canopy gave way.

He had to get air and save Cole. He would do it or die trying.

Eyes stinging from salt water, Scott shot to the surface and sucked in the welcome scent of ocean brine. Before he could dive under and rescue Cole, a large wave slammed into him. His mouth filled with seawater. He gagged and coughed it out, surprised that the salty tang was missing.

The water had a chemical taste and odor to it. Chlorine?

Before he could take in a lungful of fresh air, someone close behind him yelled, "GERONIMO!"

It was a little girl's voice.

Scott spun around, but another wave hit his face. Eyes bleary from the repeated dousing, he spat the water out, and wondered why the sky was suddenly overcast.

The voice spoke again, echoing oddly. "Hi, Scotty. I'm glad you made it."

The words sounded as if spoken inside a deserted auditorium. Watery dripping and splashing noises accompanied the voice – a little *English* girl's voice.

Scott's vision cleared, and he gasped in disbelief.

The "overcast sky" was a white tiled ceiling, held up by white tile walls with black trim. Unable to comprehend what had happened, Scott snapped his head left and right, scanning the strange surroundings with unbelieving eyes.

"This ... this is impossible. How the hell did ... I mean, no way could ..."

He was floating in a large indoor swimming pool!

A diving board rose high above the deep end of the pool, flanked by pairs of chrome-plated handrails and steps, while a children's slide dominated the shallow end. A bobbing line of cork floats separated the two areas. Arched stained glass windows, graced with art nouveau floral patterns, were mounted in all four walls. Two rows of large, Tiffany-style globe lamps hung from the ceiling. The walkway surrounding the pool had wrought-iron tables, rattan chairs and bent-wood chaises longues.

The place looked like it belonged in an exclusive 19th-century country club or a posh resort spa. But there were no members or guests or employees. No one, not a single soul – except ...

Scott looked around again. Where *had* the little girl's voice come from?

A stream of air bubbles frothed the water in front of him. Then a dark shape rose from the depths near his feet. Fearful of the shadowy form, Scott back-paddled with his arms in water tainted red from his bloody wounds. He fully expected a confrontation with a monstrous sea creature – a bloodthirsty, sharp-toothed beast with a ravenous appetite.

Scott reached for the survival knife strapped to his right leg. As he grasped the knife's handle, the phantom thing's head broke the surface and roared – in girlish laughter.

"How do you like my little old swimming hole, Scotty boy?" A girl, perhaps nine or ten years old, grinned and stuck a hand out. "I'm happy we could finally meet, but I must apologize for such short notice."

Scott, stunned and without thinking, reached out and shook her tiny hand. "What the hell is going on? I mean … who are you and how … how did I get here? And what in heaven's name is this place?"

She giggled and said, "My name is Victoria. And, for the moment, this is exactly where you need to be."

"Am … am I dead?"

"Of course not, silly. At least not if you can avoid the mistake you were about to make."

"Mistake?"

"Yes, you were ready to dive under and rescue your poor rear-seat gunner, but –"

Jolted back to reality, Scott shouted, "Gunny! My God, where is he? I gotta save him."

"Take it easy, Scotty. For you, time has temporarily stopped."

"What do you mean, 'stopped'?"

"Exactly that. You are in a personal 'time-out' period. Things will eventually resume right where they left off." Victoria doggie-paddled over to the handrails. "Follow me, please. I need to show you something," she said, and climbed out of the pool.

As Scott climbed after Victoria, he noticed her old-fashioned swim suit. She wore a short black- and purple-striped dress-like top over knee-length bloomers, with black stockings, canvas wading slippers, and a floppy purple cloth cap. Victoria looked like she'd stepped right out of a beach scene in a Charlie Chaplin or Buster Keaton silent film comedy. Scott's waterlogged and bloodstained outfit of khaki flying suit, an uninflated yellow "Mae West" life preserver, brown shoes, canvas and leather pilot's helmet, and parachute/seat pack felt only slightly more cumbersome than hers looked.

Scott looked around the pool walkway while pink-tinted water drizzled from his flight suit. He still couldn't comprehend his predicament.

"This way, Scotty," Victoria said. "We need to take the lift to the sixth floor."

When Scott glanced back at Victoria, he was shocked to see her suddenly dressed in a stylized US Army WAAC's uniform. With her tan skirt and blouse, black necktie, belt and shoes, and a folding garrison cap, she resembled a miniature version of one of the Andrews Sisters on a USO tour. He half expected her to break out singing "Boogie Woogie Bugle Boy."

Near the exit door, Victoria picked up an antique music box from one of the tables. She turned toward Scott and opened the lid. A brilliant pulse of warm, emerald-green light blinded him for several seconds.

"There, that's much better. Can't have you dripping all over the carpeting or my lift's floor, now can we?"

Victoria set the music box down and pushed through the doorway. Scott followed, surprised to find his flight gear completely dry and blood-free.

"How the hell did you ..."

"It's much too complicated to explain," Victoria said as they entered a shiny brass elevator at the end of a short hallway. She closed the door, pushed button number six and spoke softly. "You really were feeling quite the failure today, weren't you, Scotty?"

"Yeah. My squadron got shot all to hell. I was the last one able to complete the mission, and ... and I blew it." Scott let out a resigned sigh. "I failed to use the Devastator's torpedo director instrument. I didn't have time to fool with it, and dropped the Mark-13 manually. If I *had* taken the time I might have scored a hit."

"It didn't matter, Scotty."

"Bullshit." He ripped his helmet off and threw it against the lift's door. "It *does* matter. I screwed up. Most of my squadron mates are dead and I let them down." He kicked his helmet across the floor. "Aw, hell, the whole damned mission was a debacle."

"Please listen to me, Scotty. The torpedoes had serious design flaws. They were failure-prone, and that's not your fault."

"Yeah, but it still doesn't excuse *my* hasty decisions." Scott slumped against the wall and shook his head. "You know, once I got out of my sinking plane, all I could think of was rescuing Gunny. If I can save him, maybe I can live with myself in spite of this fiasco."

"That 20mm round that exploded near your left foot passed through Cole's chest first. I'm so sorry, but ... he was dead before your plane hit the ocean."

"Oh shit," Scott said, wiping a hand across his eyes. "How ... how could you possibly know that, or ... or any of these things?"

"No words can explain it. Even I'm not sure *how* it works. I only know that it does."

The lift's bell rang and button number six glowed green. "What I'm about to show you will put everything into context." Victoria took his hand in hers. "Trust me, Scotty, as dark as things appear now, there is every reason for hope. You'll see," she said as the lift's door slid open.

They stepped into what appeared to be the interior of a long Quonset hut. Corrugated steel panels curved across the ceiling and arched down to form walls at floor level. Rows of wooden folding chairs lined either side of a central aisle, which led to a desk in front of a large blackboard. The desk had several Army field telephones on it, plus a box of chalk, an eraser and a rubber-tipped wooden pointer stick. The place looked exactly like the sort of pilots' briefing and ready room Scott expected to find at Midway's naval air field on Eastern Island.

"Have a seat, Scotty. This will take a minute or two."

Victoria took a piece of chalk and approached the blackboard. At the center-bottom, she drew outlines of the atoll's Eastern and Sand Islands. In the upper right corner she drew three small rectangles, two close together and one further away. "These two represent Admiral Spruance's *Hornet* and *Enterprise* task force at 'Point Luck,' and this one is Admiral Fletcher's *Yorktown* task force nearby."

Scott was amazed that Victoria had duplicated top-secret US Navy battle plans.

Next, she drew a long line at a 45-degree angle, from the upper left corner, down toward Midway. "This is the approach course of Admiral Nagumo's Japanese carrier fleet."

Partway down, Victoria looped the line back on itself, then continued on and made two additional loops. "These are the points where Nagumo's fleet took evasive action while under attack from Midway's land-based Navy, Marine, and Army Air Force planes."

Victoria's line made a 90-degree turn and started moving upward, away from Midway. She stopped and drew an "X" on it. "This is where your squadron attacked the Japanese carriers." She continued drawing the line, making numerous curves, loops and backtracks. When Victoria finished, the line formed a large, wiggly-wormy right triangle.

She added several more "X" marks and then picked up the wooden pointer.

"When planes from Midway attacked, here and here, it threw the Japanese's carefully orchestrated plans off-base. The attacks did little or no damage, but they set the stage for what came next. Nagumo had to make numerous snap decisions, which he will come to regret. As such, your squadron's failed torpedo attack provided the key to winning the battle."

"Wait, wait, that doesn't make a damn bit of sense."

"Hear me out, Scotty. Because your torpedo runs needed to be made at such a low altitude, those fearsome Zero fighter aircraft guarding the Japanese fleet had to descend to your level."

"Yeah, that's right, but –"

"Let me finish. Even as we speak, US Navy dive bombers are about to begin their attacks from high altitude with no Japanese fighter opposition. Your torpedo squadron, plus VT-6 and VT-8, kept the Zeros down near sea level."

Victoria lowered her head for a moment and spoke in a soft voice. "It wasn't planned that way, but all three torpedo squadrons made a terrible, bloody sacrifice today. However, it is one that will make June 4th, 1942 the turning point of this war against Imperial Japan. Within a span of ten minutes, three of their carriers will be blazing wrecks. The remaining one will succumb a few hours later. All four will be on the bottom of the Pacific Ocean by tomorrow morning."

Scott closed his eyes, leaned forward, cradling his head with his hands. "All of this ... it sounds so ... so incredible. I can't believe it's possible that –" He felt a small hand on his shoulder.

"It is possible, Scotty. Everything will happen just as I said."

Scott opened his eyes and found himself seated, pool-side, in a wicker chair. Victoria stood next to him, holding his pilot's helmet in one hand and her music box in the other. She bent over and kissed his cheek.

"It's time for you to go now, Scotty. But it's *not* time for you to die. You still have a long, rewarding life to live." She handed him the helmet. "Better put this on, 'Skipper'."

"What was that mistake you said I nearly made earlier?"

"You forgot to use the quick release to jettison your parachute harness. The Devastator's tail was going to snag it and drag you under."

"I'll be sure and remember now."

"By the way, your plane's life raft and a seat cushion will pop to the surface near you. Hide under the cushion, and don't inflate the raft until the enemy fleet is gone. Otherwise they might spot you and shoot you in the water. Or they may haul you out, bind and torture you for information, then toss you back as shark food."

"I know. We were warned about their brutal treatment of POW's."

"You're going to have a very wet, ring-side seat to one of the most decisive naval battles in American history. Although you'll be in the water for the next thirty hours, don't worry. You *will* be rescued by something called a … a *'Dumbo'* … whatever that is."

"That's Navy slang for a Consolidated PBY Catalina flying boat."

"Hmm. I'm surprised *The Source* failed to mention that little detail."

"Victoria, I … I need to know something. Will I ever see you again?"

"That rarely happens. But in this case, I promise you, Scotty, I *will* be there at the very end."

With that final comment, Victoria opened the lid of her music box.

A blinding pulse of green light shot out, knocking Scott into the swimming pool.

When he surfaced, he was in the salty blue waters of the Pacific. There were aircraft roaring overhead, guns firing and bombs exploding.

The Devastator was going down nose-first, its navy-blue tail high in the air like a grave marker. Scott hit his parachute harness's quick-release coupling before the torpedo bomber's tail slipped past and disappeared into the ocean's depths.

Scott looked around and spotted a seat cushion and an uninflated rubber raft surfacing nearby, just as Victoria had predicted. When he reached for them, he

was hit by a bout of dizziness. Scott closed his eyes
for a moment and heard a strange beeping sound.

*DECEMBER 10, 2015*
*MERCY HOSPITAL*
*PITTSBURGH*

The remainder of Robert M. Scott's life shot
past his mind's eye in a mere second. He took his last
breath and the heart monitor's urgent beeping faded
into deathly silence.

Scott knew he was dead, but he certainly didn't
feel dead. In fact, he felt better than he had in years –
maybe decades.

Scott's eyes fluttered open and he could see
again. As he lay gazing upward, he marveled at just
how beautiful something as ordinary as a room's
ceiling could look. All of his bodily senses seemed to
have resumed their normal functions. No, not normal
– better than normal. A hundred times better. Even
so, he wondered why everything was so quiet. There
wasn't a sound to be heard, until –

"Hello, Scotty boy. I'll bet you thought I
wasn't going to make it in time."

Scott sat upright and knew he was no longer in
his hospital room. He could only assume that his
ornate surroundings must be the lobby of Victoria's
mysterious building.

"Yes, that's exactly where we are," she said, having apparently read his thoughts.

Victoria still had on her Andrews Sisters "uniform." As she helped Scott to his feet, he noticed he was wearing his Navy dress-white uniform. His white officer's cap was tucked neatly under his left arm. He put the cap on, took Victoria's hand, and walked with her to the lobby's main entrance.

"I'm afraid this is as far as I can go, Scotty. Your friends are waiting for you."

The twin doors swung open, and a soft, heavenly light flooded the lobby. Scott heard a familiar voice call to him from the gentle brilliance.

"Hey, Skipper, it's great to see you again."

"Gunny?"

"Yeah, it's me." Rear-seat gunner Franklin S. Cole, wearing a crisp clean flight suit, stepped out of the light. He warmly clasped Scott by the shoulder and shook his hand.

"Man, you look sharp in those dress whites. Come on, Skipper. All of the squadron guys are here, and they're anxious to greet you."

Ensign Robert M. Scott smiled and walked into the light with his friend.

Several months after Scott's funeral, his ashes were scattered in the waters of the Pacific Ocean, west-northwest of Midway Atoll. The roll call for the

three torpedo squadrons was now complete.  He was
the final one.

The Seventh Story: Treachery

# Darling Juliana
## by Scarlett R. Algee

T he trek from her parking space to the hospital's front entrance is a steep uphill climb. It's raining, she's wearing two-inch heels, and her husband is almost certainly on his way after her.

Corinna runs. She has no choice. Not after that phone call.

Corinna's in the kitchen when her cell phone rings.

She'd staggered out of bed at four-thirty this morning to make sure Eric was on his way to the airport within the hour, to catch his seven AM flight to Denver. He can't afford to miss that meeting with the board of directors, not when he's due for a promotion. She slumps at the kitchen table with her coffee as soon as he's safely out the door and that, of course, is when the ringing starts.

She scowls at the muffled chiming ringtone. She doesn't know where the thing is; after bustling to get Eric to his plane, she's lucky she knows where her head's at right now. But as she weaves into the living room and sinks into the couch to catch her breath, she feels movement between the cushions, and the ringing gets louder.

There it is. She fishes out the crystal-adorned pink case with the large letter *J* on the back, and stares at the number on the screen. It's not one she recognizes, and she starts to tap *decline*. But it's got the area code of her hometown, and that's enough to make her pause. She doesn't want to think who'd be calling from there at six in the morning, and she ignores the noise to turn the case over in her hand. It had been Eric's attempt at a gift for their last anniversary: *J for Juliana*, he'd said with glee, oblivious to the fake smile she'd plastered on at the sound of that name, the fake smile she's worn for four years. The case looks like a tween's bad attempt at Bedazzling.

The phone's still ringing. Corinna sighs; it should've gone to voicemail by now. She flips her hair back and grudgingly thumbs *accept*. "Hello."

She doesn't make it a question. The voice on the other end is male and faintly hoarse. "Hello? Corinna Lopez?"

The sound of her own name makes her grit her teeth. "Look, whoever you are, I think you have the wrong number, this is the Kenshaw residence–"

"No ma'am," he insists. "Listen, Miss Lopez, we don't have much time." He doesn't give her a chance to interrupt. "I'm Tom Reilly from Gramercy Hospital in Bentonville. It's about your sister, Juliana."

Anger blossoms hot in Corinna's chest. No. No. Not now. "I don't have a sister."

"Really?" To his credit, Tom Reilly doesn't sound surprised. "We found your name and number on a card in her wallet. Clearly labeled 'next of kin'."

Of course it would be. Corinna grabs at the couch's upholstery, digging in her nails as black encroaches on the edge of her vision.

"Corinna? Are you *sure* you don't have a sister?"

She swallows. Her mouth is dry with the aftertaste of burnt coffee. "Tell me what happened."

"Car accident. Your sister was driving drunk. I'm sorry I couldn't call sooner, but she's in emergency surgery now—"

Corinna can't bite her tongue fast enough: "Is she going to make it?"

"Maybe. We don't know yet," Reilly says. "She was lucid a little, before, and asking for you." His voice wavers a little. "You should get here as fast as you can, just in case."

"Mr. Reilly, *I'm* Juliana Lopez Kenshaw," Corinna answers, trying to cover the slip and get some kind of composure back. "I don't know what kind of sick mix-up this is, but I'm not my sister. Besides, I'm two hours away across the state line, I don't know if I can even make it, so—"

"Try." A harsh edge creeps into Tom Reilly's voice. "Miss Lopez, Mrs. Kenshaw, whatever you call yourself, she told us quite a lot before she went under. She's told us everything. So we'll do our best to keep her alive until you can get here, but you'd better hurry."

The call drops in a trio of beeps. Corinna tosses the phone aside and puts her face in her hands.

So this is it. She's finally been caught out.

She leaves the house without packing a bag.

She hadn't called Eric – still waiting to board – until she was twenty miles away on the interstate. Corinna reaches the hospital entrance, and stops to catch her breath as she mentally replays her half of the conversation.

*Look, baby, don't freak out, but I have to run back home. It's my sister, there's been an accident... Yeah, Corinna. No. Eric, no. You can't miss that meeting, and I'll be fine. The staff guy who called said she was asking for me, so she's talking, it can't be that bad. Probably just shook her up and tore up the car. You know how she always was. Of course I'll let you know as soon as I find out something. Just don't fall out of the sky, okay?* It was the closest thing they had to an in-joke. *I love you too. Be safe.*

She checks her phone. No calls; no texts. That's good, right?

Just as Corinna's about to step close enough to trigger the automatic doors, a nurse comes strolling out into the cool morning air. There are dark splatters on her dull lavender scrubs, and Corinna starts to approach her, question her, when the woman's hair catches her eye. It's red, red like a carrot, red like–

–the doll Juliana had gotten for their seventh birthday, long red curls framing a porcelain-perfect face, big blue eyes that closed or opened as she was moved, checkered blue gingham dress and neat black shoes with white stockings. Corinna had picked at her cake, sullenly clutching the sidewalk chalk set that was her own present (*Corrie's too clumsy to be trusted with anything so delicate,* their mom had said), and something had shifted in her, made her snap her plastic fork down and lunge at Juliana, punch her sister in the face and snatch the doll, bolt up the stairs to their shared bedroom and hide under her bed with her stolen prize, hot tears of rage streaking her face as her parents' shouts drifted up from downstairs. "It's not fair," she'd said to herself. "Julie always gets the best stuff, it's not fair, it's not–"

"It's not fair," Corinna whispers in the here and now, making the nurse turn back and eye her quizzically. She steps forward as the double doors slide open, wafting out the tang of tile cleaner and stale cafeteria food. "It's never been fair."

She's going to be in trouble. She's going to be in so much trouble.

Corinna makes it inside to the lobby, and stops to stare.

This doesn't look like the hospital she remembers from having her appendix out at twelve. The smell is right, bleach and wax and day-old fried chicken, but the look is all wrong. Gramercy Hospital's never been this *clean*, never had wicker furniture and fronded plants in brass pots, never had a parquet floor she could see her reflection in.

Never been this quiet.

She scans the space. No one else is here. There's faint noise just on the edge of her hearing – voices, machines beeping – but no one at all sitting at the admission cubicles or in the wicker chairs, when there ought to be at least a couple dozen people in here, overflow from the ER waiting room. *They've remodeled,* she thinks. It's the sort of thing her mother would have loved.

Somewhere nearby, a man clears his throat, grabbing Corinna's attention. She follows the sound to an information desk, long and polished, looking like something out of a 1920s hotel. The man sitting behind it is tall and slim, with sandy hair and pale blue eyes; at the sight of her, he lays down the book he's reading. "Corinna Lopez?" he asks, and adds, "The truth, please."

Corinna can't stifle a huff. "Fine. Yes. Though it really is Kenshaw, if you must know." She eyes him uncertainly. "Are you Tom Reilly? Can you tell me anything about my sister? Is she–"

"One thing at a time," he answers, smiling, but not enough for it to reach his eyes. "I'm Tom, yes. Miss Lopez came out of recovery forty minutes ago; I tried to call, but it never rang on your end. Anyway, she's in a room; kind of in and out, you understand, given the anesthesia, but she's still with us. Still asking for you." Tom gets to his feet, gesturing for her to follow him. "Let me show you the way. You'll have a lot to talk about, I'm sure."

Corinna's too numb to do anything but nod, until he leads her past the clearly-marked elevators. "Wait. Don't tell me she's down here on the first floor."

Tom shakes his head. "Just follow me. Consider this a shortcut to where you need to be."

She frowns, but follows him. There's a left turn past the elevators that leads to a back hallway, and here the shiny newness stops. The sage paint is flaking in spots and the parquet has given way to worn brown carpet. Must be where the remodeling money had run out. "Do you work here?" Corinna asks.

"I'm a volunteer." Tom leads her around another corner, and they're standing in front of an elevator Corinna's never seen before.

The outer doors are ornate openwork bronze. It's in keeping with the "old hotel" look, only without the polish. The inner doors are open, and the light inside has a greenish cast. Corinna has to wonder if it's safe; the whole thing looks rickety. "Mr. Reilly – Tom? Is this some kind of secret staff elevator?"

"If you like." It's not Tom who answers, but a little girl, stepping out of the dim, open elevator car. She can't be more than nine or ten, if Corinna's guessing right; the green light casts odd highlights on the child's blonde curls and gleams on her black patent shoes. Her dress, purple and frilled as if it's made to match the retro renovation, stops a bit below her knees. "Tommy. You got her here. Good. Just in time, too."

*You got her here.* What's that mean? "What the hell," Corinna says.

"Excuse me. Did you say something, Mrs. Kenshaw? Corinna. May I call you Corinna?" The girl executes a neat little bow. "Oh, where are my manners? Call me Victoria. I'm here to take you the rest of the way."

"To my sister?" Corinna demands. "You? What, this place lets kids volunteer now?"

Behind her, Tom murmurs, "Victoria's not quite what she seems, Corinna." Then he adds, to the girl, "Need me to come along?"

Victoria smiles and shakes her head, making her curls bob. "No, Tommy, thank you. You get back to your reading; I'll take Mrs. Kenshaw from here." She cocks her head in Corinna's direction. "Or is it Corinna? You never said."

"That's...that's fine." Corinna has to get the words out between her teeth. "Look, what kind of act is this? I'm here to see my sister, damn it, not waste time."

Tom walks away, back the way they'd come. "It's no act, Corinna," Victoria says pleasantly, though her expression is calculating and shrewd, far older than the child she seems to be. "Time works a little differently right now. You see, Juliana's been quite vocal about you, when she could be. So I've decided you need a little time to think about some of the things you've done before you see her. Or, more importantly, before your husband sees her."

Eric. Corinna's heart sinks, and she grabs for her phone. Still no messages or missed calls. Good. If he's decided to be foolish and come after her, he hasn't caught up yet.

Victoria gestures for Corinna to enter the elevator. "Follow me, please." She catches Corinna's skeptical look and holds out a hand. "Please. I assure you the lift is perfectly safe, and besides, from what your sister says, you probably have quite a few things to reflect on. So let's not, as you say, waste time."

Corinna walks grudgingly into the car, trying not to scowl again. The floor feels perfectly solid under her feet, even if there's no inspection certificate she can see. The outer doors close first, squeaking faintly, then the inner ones, sealing her in with this weird kid and the strange green light. "Look, little girl, whoever you are," she begins, "about Juliana, we were kids, okay?"

She stops for a moment, because the light's intensified, and she's just realized that Victoria is the source of the light – or something she's holding is. It's a wooden box of some kind, one Corinna hadn't noticed before. "What's that?"

"My music box." Victoria opens the lid a little and the green light becomes a glow, briefly, before an unfamiliar tune begins to play. She closes the lid, and the music softens but doesn't stop. "But I believe you were trying to say something."

"I. Yeah. About Juliana. Look, whatever she's told you, I know I wasn't always the kindest sister. But it's hard being twins, you know? And anyway, kids are mean."

Victoria's lips thin as she studies the elevator's buttons, and a spasm of something crosses her face for just an instant before her expression resumes porcelain smoothness. "Yes. I know. But you didn't let it stop there, did you? Seventh floor." She says the last two words almost absently, pushing a button. The car jolts and begins to move.

"Wait," Corinna objects. "What do you mean, seventh floor? This hospital doesn't *have* a seventh floor."

Victoria gives her a long look. "For you it does." She leans back against the side of the car, watching the panel light up as they climb floors, slender arms crossed protectively over her music box. The five lights up, then the six. "Almost there. Tell me, Corinna, do you remember the butterflies?"

✳ ✳ ✳

Of course Corinna remembers the damned butterflies. She'd laughed about it to herself for weeks just because it had been so simple.

Fifth grade. They'd been ten, not yet eleven, and the six-week science project for their class had been collecting insects on foam board and labeling them correctly. Their teacher, Mrs. Wallace, had been clear about the rules: exactly fifty bugs for an A, forty to forty-nine for a B, and so on. Bonus points for collecting butterflies.

Corinna had dutifully scoured the yards in the neighborhood: a praying mantis, a grape leaf skeletonizer off the next door neighbor's Muscat vine, two species of ticks from her aunt's dog, three carefully-caught wasps from the back porch. She'd built the bulk of her fifty-insect collection on easily found specimens, on flies and beetles and the moths drawn by the porch light.

Juliana, of course, had picked a few bugs from the back yard, but had begged their dad to take her butterfly hunting. So it was off to the park and the zoological gardens, armed with a net and an identification book, with a box of half-pint Mason jars stashed in the van. And by the time her foam board was full, she'd accumulated ten butterflies for her bottom row, including a few her parents had never seen before, all labeled in her neatest handwriting.

Corinna's chance had come on the day the assignment was due. They were twenty minutes early, trying to carefully wrangle their foam boards full of delicate cargo out of the van before everyone else showed up, when Mrs. Mullers from the PTA had come up to the front passenger window.

"Angelica?" she'd said to their mom. "Can I have a quick word with Julie? It's about Girl Scouts."

Juliana had just eased her insects out of the back seat, and had frozen. "Mom, I don't know, I need to take this to Mrs. Wallace..."

"I'll take it." Corinna shifted her backpack, dangling her own project from one hand. "I can take both of them, Julie, you go ahead." Corinna never got talked to about Girl Scouts.

"I don't know..." Juliana frowned, biting her lip. But Mrs. Mullers cleared her throat impatiently and Julie said, "Okay, okay, go ahead." She passed her foam board to her sister, shouting at her immediately retreating back, "Be careful, Corrie!"

And oh, Corinna was indeed careful. Careful to go immediately to the girls' bathroom on the sixth-grade hall and quickly, steadily, use her house key to scrape the butterflies off Juliana's foam board and into a toilet. She peeled the little labels off with her nails, flushed the lot, washed her hands and took the boards to their classroom.

Mrs. Mullers didn't ask questions: she just counted bugs. Juliana had to settle for a B and a scolding from her parents, and a withdrawal of the promised Girl Scouts membership. Corinna, meanwhile, had just gloated quietly in her A.

"And that" – Victoria's voice cuts into Corinna's memory – "that was worth hurting her, somehow?"

Corinna glances at her, then looks away. The tinkle from that music box is starting to grate on her nerves. "You don't understand. We were identical. Supposed to be alike in every way. I busted my ass in school, I did the best I could, but Mom and Dad still insisted that *Juliana* was smarter, *Juliana* was more talented – I dropped a vase when I was three and my mother called me 'too clumsy' till the day she died."

There's a dulcet note as they reach the seventh floor, and the elevator slowly glides to a stop. The doors open: first the inner, then the outer. Corinna stares out into another long sage-walled hallway; at the far end she can see a door, the faintest hint of green light seeping out from beneath it. "That's it, huh."

"This is it," Victoria agrees. "You might want to start thinking about your apologies now, Corinna.

There's no reason to be beastly to your sister."

Corinna just shrugs her off and steps out. Speckled tile this time, not parquet or carpet. "Girls are mean," she says. "It's easy. Besides, I was just keeping her humble."

The hallway's longer than it looks, as though it's some kind of optical illusion. Victoria's firmly leading Corinna by one hand, so Corinna, not wanting to look ahead at the strangely lit door, not wanting to think about what shape her sister might be in, focuses her gaze on the tile floor. They'd had tile like this on the floor of the Sunday school classroom she and Juliana had shared at twelve, when it was early December and time to make props for the annual Christmas play.

Neither of them had attained the coveted role of the Virgin Mary; that had gone to the blonde girl who'd just moved to town, who was two grades ahead. So while the adults handled sewing the costumes, Juliana had been assigned to make glittery poster board wings for the play's three angels – of which she was one – while Corinna, who hadn't been cast, had been handed a stack of white paper and a pair of kindergarten safety scissors, and told to make snowflakes. *There weren't any snowflakes in Bethlehem,* she told herself sourly as she snipped centers and trimmed corners, wishing she'd been let do something with markers or pastels or even regular scissors, instead.

164

She offered to stay late that morning to clean up, earning herself a grateful smile from their teacher, Miss Bonaventura. Nobody else, not even perfect Juliana, wanted to volunteer to clean up all that excess glitter.

It was all the chance she needed.

The class agreed to meet the next Saturday, to make sure they had everything they needed before Sunday night's rehearsal. Corinna had arrived on her bike a few minutes ahead of her sister, and had just settled into an empty classroom with some fresh poster board when Juliana burst in.

"Corinna! We can't find my wings! Where are my wings?"

Corinna just bent over her work: laying down carefully constructed swirls of glue, then applying glitter. "Do I look like I've seen your stupid wings? I got stuck making snowflakes like a baby!"

"I know you've seen them! I know you!" Juliana grabbed the back of her chair and shook it hard. "What did you do with my wings?"

It was almost a wail. Corinna sighed theatrically and shoved her chair back, pushing Juliana out of the way. "Okay, okay, I saw your stupid angel wings," she admitted. "I threw them away last Sunday when I was cleaning up."

"Threw them away!" Juliana squeaked, then lunged to get a handful of Corinna's hair, but her sister dodged and pushed her away. "Corrie, damn it, I worked hard on those–"

She clapped a hand over her mouth, realizing she'd just sworn in a church building. Corinna laughed

165

and scooted her chair back up to the table.

"Sis, really? I did you a favor, yours were crap anyway." Corinna flipped her hair back and bent to her work again. "I can make way better ones."

* * *

"And did you?" Victoria asks.

Corinna stops to catch her breath. How long is this hallway? The creepy room doesn't look any closer, but when she glances back, she can't see the elevator. "They got used. What can I say?"

Victoria gives her a hard sidelong look. "For an intelligent woman, you've been awfully petty."

"It's gotten me what I wanted." Corinna shrugs. "That makes it worthwhile. How much farther, anyway? Am I seeing my sister today?"

Victoria shrugs too, mirroring her motion delicately. "You still have things to talk about."

Corinna stops. "Why? Why do I have to talk about anything? Your friend 'Tommy' said Julie told you everything."

"She did," Victoria answers brightly. "And it'll do you no end of good to hear yourself saying it." She bends down and plucks something from the floor; it's a lengthy, slightly crinkled strip of shiny gold plastic, torn from a pom-pom. "Why don't you tell me about the cheerleading tryouts?"

Corinna huffs. That, really, was when things had maybe started getting out of hand. Maybe. "Why don't I."

* * *

They were in the last two weeks of eighth grade when cheerleading tryouts took place. Corinna was scheduled for one week, Juliana the next; the girls who got selected would make the team for their first year of high school, and the teenage prestige that came with being on the roster rivaled that saved for the football team.

But there was no prestige when Corinna fell off the top of the three-person pyramid and broke her ankle. There was just going to the ER for a cast and then going home to sulk.

They were both up past their bedtime, that night. Corinna scribbled half-heartedly at her take-home American history exam, while Juliana giggled over her phone as she texted her friends about the upcoming week of tryouts. "This is gonna be great," she said to herself.

"Seriously?" Corinna looked up from her notebook to glare first at her cast, then at her sister. "We've done everything together and now you're trying out for cheer without me?"

Juliana put the phone down and rolled her eyes. "Come on, Corrie. You had an accident. I'm sorry it happened, and yeah, I'd rather be on the squad with you, but am I just supposed to put the rest of my life on hold now? We're about to be in high school. Then we're going to college. At some point you've got to get out of my shadow."

*She thinks I'm holding her back*, Corinna realized,

and it stung. She levered herself off the bed, wincing when her cast bumped the floor, and dragged herself across the room to Juliana's bed. She reached up and grabbed her sister's pajama bottoms, yanking, hearing pajamas and panties rip as she pulled Juliana onto the carpet. "Maybe you want to be in my shadow for once, huh?"

Juliana's head bounced off the floor. "Ow! Corrie! What's wrong with you?"

"You are! Do you know what it's been like, spending my entire life hearing I'm not as good as you?"

"Corrie, that's not true–"

"The hell it's not!" Corinna's hands curled into fists, and she slammed one into Juliana's shoulder. The soft wet *snap* of bone seemed too loud.

Juliana howled. "Bitch!"

That did it. Footsteps stomped up the stairs, and their mother slammed the door open, snarling. "*What is going on in here?*"

The twins looked at each other, and started to get up slowly. "We were just," Corinna began lamely.

"Tickle fighting," Juliana finished.

"One of you's got a broken ankle and you're *tickle fighting?*" Angelica Lopez scoffed at her daughters as they retreated to their respective beds, Juliana doing her best not to rub her collarbone. "What's *wrong* with you two..." She huffed. "Finish your damned homework and go the hell to bed!"

She disappeared with another slam of the door. Corinna reached down for her notebook, which had fallen on the floor. Juliana fiddled with her phone, one hand to her shoulder, sniffling. After a moment, she threw the phone down, rolled away from Corinna to face the nearest wall, and yelped as she immediately regretted it.

"If I can't be on the cheer squad," Corinna said casually, "neither will you."

Juliana was silent for about ten seconds; then she sniffled loudly. "I hate you."

Corinna just giggled and turned back to her history textbook. "I know."

✳ ✳ ✳

"So there's your story," Corinna says sullenly, though truth be told, she still laughs inwardly at the memory of the next morning: how Juliana had pretended to be fine until she'd had to pick up her backpack. The scream she'd let out had been worth a few weeks of grounding. "Do you want to hear more? Since it seems I'm trapped here all day."

"Trapped?" Victoria asks. "Is that what you think? I'm offering you a chance to reflect so you can do better. Think of it as a second chance so you and your sister can make up. Because, believe me, you don't want to see the alternative."

This doesn't even sound weird anymore. None of it: not the odd little girl, not the spooky elevator, not even the gently glowing music box that's still playing softly. Corinna sighs. "We got separate bedrooms after that. Locks on the doors. Didn't give me a chance to do much." For the first time in years, she realizes, she can hear regret in her own voice. "Although..."

"You're volunteering another story? That's a good sign." Victoria smiles encouragingly, and when Corinna falls silent, the girl prompts, "Although?"

"Yeah." Suddenly the door at the end of the hall seems closer, and Corinna shivers. "There was that one thing at the end of high school."

Weird, Corinna reflected, that her mother had to send her upstairs to fetch out her sister. Usually she was the oversleeping one, and Juliana was up by daybreak. Shrugging, she shouldered the bedroom door open without knocking. "Hey, lazy ass, come on, we're gonna be late."

Juliana lay still tangled in the sheets, making a pained noise. "Corrie? I need your help."

Corinna scoffed. "My help? *You*? You must be kidding, what's wrong with you?"

"I need you to pretend to be me. To – to take my trig test." Juliana lifted her head enough to see Corinna's incredulous look, then let it flop back. "Don't look at me like that. I know we've never switched on our teachers before, but I just can't go. I've started...you know... Corrie, I took six ibuprofen overnight and I'm still cramping. I had to crawl to the bathroom."

Corinna wrinkled her nose. "Jeez, Julie, can't you just ask Mom for a hot water bottle or something?"

She opened the closet door and started picking through her sister's clothes. "I mean, okay, you'd have to miss the first two classes or something, but you'd be all right by exam time."

"That requires *moving*." Juliana curled herself into a tighter knot on the bed and hissed between her teeth. "And I'm not asking Mom to write a note to the principal telling him I missed class because of my stupid period. Everybody'd *know*." She tried to sit up and fails miserably, clutching at her lower belly. "It's just a math test, okay? Even you can handle a math test."

"Oh, low blow." Corinna plucked a grey blouse from its hanger and turned to glare at her sister. "Okay, say I do this. I change into *your* clothes after gym class and go into *your* trig section and take *your* exam. What do I get out of it?"

Juliana writhed for a silent few seconds, then grated out, "I'll take your English exam next week. I know I can ace that."

Corinna studied her, chewing her lower lip. The English exam was technically the final for her section – Mr. Patrelli was leaving before the end of the school year, some health issue or other – but she wasn't sure Juliana was aware of all the details. "There's the essay that's due first."

Juliana turned over, burying her face in her pillow. "Subject?"

"Something about Shakespeare? I don't have it all planned, I just have some notes down."

Juliana swore into the pillow. "Fine. Fine. I can't

get out of bed, and I can't be valedictorian without an A on that math test, and for that I need you. So exam, essay, which is it?"

Corinna turned back to the closet and found the skirt that matched the blouse. "Both." She watched her sister start to protest and cut her off: "Oh, no. You want to be valedictorian, right? And you want my help? You have to pay for it."

"Then what happened?" Victoria prompts quietly.

"Don't you know all this? I bombed, of course. Not entirely on purpose, either. We were in two different sections of the same trigonometry class – how was I supposed to know her teacher was three chapters ahead of mine?" Corinna grins nervously. "All right, fine. We had the same damned textbook, I knew Julie worked ahead, I could've kept up and done better. But hey, my grades were good too. Bumping Juliana out of the top spot was just putting myself in it."

Victoria says nothing, but her gaze is positively withering. Corinna shivers and looks away.

"I finally surpassed her," she says. "After all those years of trying. And it should've been enough. But it wasn't. It still wasn't."

Victoria's music box isn't so much playing now as leaking notes at intervals, a soft distorted dirge. "Apparently not. Because you could've let it end there, Corinna, and you didn't. You could have stopped this at any time. There's this little thing called honesty."

She takes the woman's hand, tugging her further down the hall toward the room at the end. The green light is leaking out all around the door now. "I think it's time we talked about Eric."

Corinna winces. "I'd rather not."

Victoria studies her. "Really. Why not?"

"Because that–" Is she choking up? "That was the last time I saw her, until now. And if Eric's possibly on his way, then...I don't have the faintest idea what to tell him."

"Pangs of conscience beginning to prick you at last?" There's a touch of acid in Victoria's voice, though her tone is gentle. They're close enough to the door now that either of them could reach out and touch it, and the girl makes an impatient gesture. "Eric. If you please."

Eric.

He and Juliana had met in their last year of college. He was rangy and rawboned, with a permanent tan and a shock of black hair: a cattleman's son from out of state, first in his family to attempt anything beyond high school. Corinna had disliked him on sight. So had their parents.

So Juliana, of course, had fallen in love.

Two days after their graduation, Juliana was pacing her bedroom at twelve in the afternoon, with a folder of paperwork on her dresser and a suitcase open on her bed. She turned to Corinna, who was leaning in the doorway watching with a smirk, and asked, "Is Dad still asleep?"

Corinna snorted. "It's Dad. He's drunk. He'll sleep till dinner. Mom won't be home from her garden club thing till four." She picked up the folder and glanced through the contents: driver's license, Social Security card, birth certificate, passport. "So you're really going through with this, huh."

"I just need to get a few things packed. Not much." Juliana sat on the edge of her bed and twisted the engagement ring on her finger, the one she'd hidden from their parents. "I can't wait for them to approve, Corrie, it has to be now. We have to be in Toledo before Monday so Eric can start his new job."

Her twin laughed at that. "I still can't believe you turned a cowboy into a marketing genius." But Corinna caught her sister's hand, staring at her fingers. "Good God, you're shaking."

"I'm so nervous," Juliana admitted. "I don't know what to pack, I can't concentrate, I..."

"Hey, hey, chill." Corinna got up and opened the closet door. "Look, you need a Valium? Mom left her purse."

"I – yeah. Yeah, that would be great." Juliana put her face in her hands for a moment, breathing deeply. "Then...Corrie...do you think you could help me pack? I know you hate me, but you're all I have right now. Till Eric gets here, anyway."

He was coming by to get her at two. Corinna forced a smile out of her scowl. "I don't hate you, dumbass, you just piss me off all the time. It's what sisters are for. Hold tight."

Corinna found the Valium in her mom's purse, right enough, but when she reached in to replace the bottle, she encountered another. Curious, she pulled it out.

Ambien. Perfect. She shook out two.

When she returned to the room with the Valium in one hand and a glass of orange juice in the other, Juliana was sitting on the bed again, twisting her hands together, but at least she'd made a little progress. There were three shirts and two pairs of jeans in the suitcase. "What took you so long? And you know I hate orange juice."

Corinna shrugged. "The tap water looked rusty. Besides, I had to get the vodka from the liquor cabinet, and Dad kept mumbling like he was waking up. I had to be careful."

Juliana looked up with her mouth full of orange juice; she'd already swallowed the Valium. "Vodka? You put vodka in this?"

"Just a teaspoon, Julie, don't have a fit. Putting the bottle back was the hard part." No, actually, crushing the Ambien had been the hard part; the makeshift screwdriver was just an attempt to mask the taste. "Go on, drink your juice. The vitamin C's good for stress." Corinna moved back to the closet, picking up clothes with no objection from her sister. "Thinking I hate you. Hah. So, what? Cowboy's gonna drive up in his farm truck and you're gonna climb out the window?"

That got an actual laugh from Juliana. "Oh God, no. I don't want to break anything *else*." She gave Corinna a meaningful look, set the empty glass on the dresser, and came to lean over her sister's shoulder. "Grab my black pumps, would you? I'm not wasting space with too many shoes, I'll just take those and what I have on. Oh, and get that black tank top with the floral print, too."

Corinna just did as she was told. "Put those in the suitcase and let me grab socks. You'll need socks."

Fifteen minutes later, when the suitcase was half full, Juliana sat down on the bed heavily. "Oh, I don't feel good."

Corinna stepped over, touching her forehead. "What's wrong?"

"Don't know." Juliana shook her head and nearly fell over. "Just...tired. Weird."

"It's the Valium," Corinna pronounced. "Plus, all the adrenaline in your system. You know, I should hate *you*, I'm the one being left to explain this to Mom and Dad." She glanced at the clock – not even one, yet – and patted Juliana on the shoulder. "Julie. Just put your head back, okay? I know how to pack clothes."

"But..."

"Don't worry, I got this. You get a nap, I'll wake you up as soon as Eric shows."

"Oh, you're the best," Juliana declared, and it came out *besht*. She leaned forward and hugged Corinna clumsily. "You're the best. I forgive you. I forgive you for everything."

She lay back. Five minutes later, she was

snoring. Corinna watched her for a few seconds, then scooped up the folder of documents and tucked it into the suitcase. She zipped the case, and Juliana didn't react to the noise.

Eric pulled into the driveway at one forty-five. Corinna bent to the bed, drew the engagement ring off Juliana's finger and slipped it on her own – of course it fit perfectly – then grabbed the suitcase and headed toward the stairs, the front door, and then on to Toledo.

"And he's never known," Victoria says.

Corinna shakes her head. "He's never known."

"And he calls you by her name."

"Why wouldn't he? I hate it." Corinna puts her hand on the doorknob at last. She stares at the floor, saturated with green light spilling out from under the door. "So. This is it. I just go in?"

"You just go in," Victoria agrees. "What happens after that is up to you."

Corinna opens the door and steps inside, and everything changes at once. The emerald light diffuses, sinking into the dull sage of the walls. She glances at her phone – only fifteen minutes have passed since she entered the hospital. How's that possible? She'd spent hours in that hallway, surely. She glances back at Victoria; the girl has slipped into the room behind her, tucking herself into the shadows behind the door. The music box has slowed to infrequent notes now, blending in with the low beeps of the machines.

So many machines. So many tubes and wires. Heart monitor. Oxygen mask. Bandages. Saline. Blood. Corinna leans over the bed to get a look at Juliana's face, and the sight makes her heart clog her throat. There's blood crusted around Juliana's nostrils, and a thin line of black sutures across her forehead.

The door squeaks open. Corinna cringes, expecting her husband, but it's just another nurse, checking all the readings and making notes on a napkin. "You kin?" she asks, talking right over Juliana, not looking at Corinna at all. "Don't know about this one. Heard it's her third or fourth DUI, finally caught up to her. Never was the same after her folks died and her sister ran off. Still, what can you do."

The nurse finishes scribbling and walks out, thumping the door shut. Corinna doesn't touch Juliana, not yet. She's too busy studying the EKG and all the equipment, automatically wondering what to disconnect. Pushing the thought from her mind is an effort.

"I caused this," she whispers. "I caused this, didn't I."

"Yes," Victoria whispers back, and Juliana opens her eyes.

"You...came," she manages.

"You called." Corinna tries to smile, but tears leak from her eyes instead. "How could I not?"

Juliana nods; she's drifting. Her eyes close, and

the sharp spikes of her EKG begin to soften. Corinna jumps up and shakes her. "You're not dying on me, dammit! You forgave me, Juliana! You said you forgave me! Breathe!"

"You said...take care of things." Juliana speaks without opening her eyes. "You lied. So can...can I." She takes a breath with an effort, making the line of her EKG spike high, and opens her eyes, staring Corinna in the face. "You never liked to share."

Someone knocks on the door, and it opens before Corinna can answer. It's Eric, his suit rumpled and rain-streaked. There's no sign of Victoria, and Corinna realizes the music has stopped entirely. She's on her own. "Eric–"

"Eric," Juliana echoes.

"Corinna?" He looks between the two of them, wild-eyed. "My God, Cor – Juliana?" His gaze shifts to his wife. "Julie, honey? Julie, why aren't you saying anything?"

Corinna reaches to grasp Juliana's hand, watching her sister's ECG slump and flatten. She takes a deep breath and doesn't look at her husband.

"Eric," she says, "there's something I need to tell you."

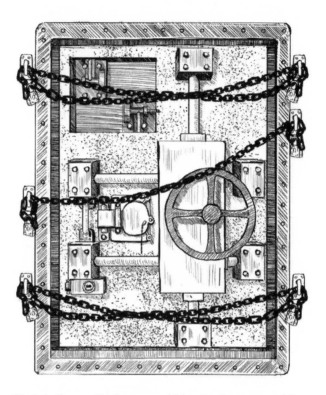

The Eighth Story: Dishonesty / Lies by Omission / Secrecy

# Human Monsters
## by Lee A. Forman

As I unlocked the door, I heard familiar shuffling on the other side. It made me think of how when you know someone is about to enter the room, your posture adjusts in preparation, as if it mattered. Even Barry did it.

*No fixing that posture,* I thought, but felt the sting of guilt soon after. *It's not his fault he looks that way.*

Barry sat in the middle of his room, hands – if you could call them that – fumbling with one another. His large eye looked up at me; the small one looked down in shame. I hated how he always had to stare at me with the big fucked-up one.

I wiped an accumulation of dirt off my clothes, patting out as much as I could. "Awful dust storm out there today."

Barry replied with little more than a low grumble.

"Come on, don't be like that," I said, removing my jacket and hanging it on the rusted steel hook near the single metal door that served as both entrance and exit. "Look," I said, displaying canned food I'd 'obtained'. "I got some good stuff today."

Barry huffed. "I'm tired of all that stuff, Sherman. It's pretty much all you ever find."

I dropped the cans on the floor. "Well, I'm sorry if the hell out there doesn't have much of a selection. We're lucky to find food at all. So which one do you want? Meatballs with spaghetti, beans, or carrots?"

"If I have to eat any more beans I'll kill myself," Barry said. "Meatballs, I guess."

I lit the gas stove and dumped the can into a pot. The aroma filled the bunker. I'd always hated the damn things. I was grateful Barry favored them.

"So what was it like today?" Barry asked as he climbed into his custom raised chair at our dining table. "See anyone else?"

"I never see anyone. You know that."

"I know," Barry sighed. "I just hope maybe one day you'll say yes."

"The dust storm was bad. I had to hide under a fallen house."

"What was it like to live in a house?" Barry fumbled with his appendages. "I don't remember."

I thought about how to answer. I didn't want to pique too much curiosity from his already wandering imagination. It was too risky; he might demand to go out there...

"It was a lot like this," I said. "To be honest, it wasn't much different, only we had more food."

"But what about life? What was it like?"

The muscles in my hands tensed. I never liked to offer too much information. "I've told you so many times, there really isn't much more to tell."

"But I like hearing about it."

*I'm sure you do, Barry,* I thought, *and I wish I could tell you all about it.*

I stirred the hot canned meal in the cooking pot and poured a generous helping onto Barry's plate.

"Aren't you hungry?" he asked.

I'd already eaten, and certainly didn't want to stuff crap down my throat. But I had to dine with him most of the time. I couldn't claim loss of appetite for too many meals.

"Not really, but I guess I should eat something." I poured a small amount onto my own plate.

We sat at the little two-person dining table attached to one of the bunker walls. I stirred the food on my plate while he shamelessly dug in.

Barry slammed his fork onto the table. "Why aren't you eating?" He stared; all I saw was that one large eye.

"It's rough out there. I know the fear of starvation is always there, but seeing, remembering everything that's gone... Sometimes it just makes me sick."

His oddly-shaped iris peered down. "I'm sorry. I don't mean to pester you."

"Don't apologize. I know you're only hard on me because you care."

"You're all I've got," Barry said, a sad yet joyful look changing his face. "Without you, I'd be dead. But even if it weren't for that, I'd still care. You're my brother. Family."

I forced a smile. "Yes...family."

\* \* \*

That night dreams of my younger brother kept me conscious in spite of sleep. He writhed in his own excreta in a barren room with no windows; a dim bulb hung from the ceiling, the only thing to light his piss- and shit-covered flesh. Grunts of misery echoed against the filthy lime-green walls.

I reached out to help him, pull him from that squalid place...but I hesitated. My fingers curled inward as I drew back, stepping in reverse as I watched the door close and the light flicker and go out.

I left him in that dark nightmare, alone.

\* \* \*

When the alarm clock woke me, I wished I could have stayed in the bunker all day. I didn't want to go out and face the world, yet it was also my escape from Barry. I sat up and rubbed my eyes, placed my bare feet on the thin carpet. I hoped I could just get ready and get out while Barry was asleep, but that was a wish denied on a daily basis. He was always there, waiting.

"Good morning, Sherman."

"Morning, Barry," I replied, closing the door to my room behind me.

"What's for breakfast?" He hopped up and down, hope in that big eye of his that it might be something better than usual.

"Don't get excited. It's just canned fruit again."

"I'm so sick of that," he sighed. "I wish there was more, like how you say it used to be."

"I know, Barry. Me too. Tell you what, I'll try extra hard to find something special for you when I go out to scavenge today."

"Really?" He hopped up and down, an unsightly gesture.

"Really," I answered. "I'm sure I can find something if I look hard enough."

Barry bounced with delight over to the dining table. He climbed up into his raised chair and prepared himself for the morning meal. I opened some canned pears, wondering what I might get for him. Something good, different, but not too obvious; nothing that would destroy the illusion.

I tried not to engage in conversation while we ate breakfast, but Barry never shut up.

"What do you think it's like outside today?" he asked.

"Won't know till I get out there."

"I want to go with you."

*Fuck. He wants to go.* "You know you can't."

"But why?" Barry's face pleaded with disappointment.

"It's too dangerous. You don't know what's out there."

"You always say there's *nothing* out there."

"Nothing worthwhile," I replied.

"It's worthwhile to me."

I dropped my fork on the plate. "Dammit, Barry. You just can't go. It'll slow me down. No offense, but I intend to stay alive out there."

"But what if you die out there? I'll be left here all alone. I'd rather die with you."

I tried not to think of it, but what *would* happen if I did die by some random accident or came down with a terminal illness? What would happen to him? Would he be found? Would he starve to death? Or would he just kill himself if I failed to come home one day? *Oh God, the shame...*

My eyes met with Barry's. "Listen, you don't know what you're saying. It'd be much worse than you think to go out there and die. It wouldn't be quick. It certainly wouldn't be painless. Think of your worst nightmares and consider it worse than that."

That damn eye of his looked deep into me, its thick eyelid closed halfway, and he replied, "My worst nightmare is dying in *here*."

I didn't know what to say to that, so I said nothing. Neither did he. We pretended to eat in tandem, pushing food around on our plates but not consuming.

"I've got to head out," I said. "Want to get an early start so I can find you something special."

Barry only nodded, wearing a sad expression.

I turned the heavy wheel that opened the bunker door, pulled it on its well-oiled hinges, and closed it, leaving shame at my back. I hurried up the steps that led to another door, this one locked, the only key on a chain around my neck – my only way of keeping Barry from leaving the bunker.

Locking the door behind me, I went up the basement stairs and into my home. Even though it was an escape from that underground hamster cage, it didn't feel like home – it felt more like the façade than the true lie. I had to spend my nights underground to keep the fabrication alive. My true home was underground with that thing I called my brother. My house had the appeal of the barren wasteland I'd described to Barry countless times. Sometimes I even believed it myself. But reality always came back when I turned on the lights and felt hot water from the shower on my musty body; when I put clean, normal clothes on my back, as opposed to the tattered rags I wore when going underground.

The lie had become my godforsaken life.

I opened the refrigerator to make a decent breakfast, but didn't find my appetite. Instead, I found my gut filled with disgust and acidic guilt. I slammed the door shut and headed upstairs to get ready for work.

In the shower, I repeated the same train of thought that plagued me daily. *Could Barry somehow get the lock open and get out? What if he did? How would I explain it?* I always tried to push aside the thoughts that followed, deny their existence. But they shoved back, and most times they won. *I'd have to put him out of his misery and bury his little corpse. Bury it and try to forget.* I hated imagining the one-man funeral. I didn't even know what I'd say, if anything at all.

*  *  *

The building was quiet when I arrived at work. My footsteps echoed in the wide-open reception area. Normally it would be full of chatter. Doris sat at her desk, staring blankly at the computer monitor. No one seemed to be talking. The usual white noise of morning conversation was absent from the air. It disturbed me. And of course, my thoughts went to Barry.

*What if he got out, and everyone here knows about it, and that's why it's so quiet? They're just waiting for the police to get here, and I'll be arrested.*

I told myself it was only paranoia, a common and expected psychosis considering my position. Considering...Barry.

The elevator sat empty when the doors slid open. I stepped in and pressed the button for the third floor. Just before the doors closed, everything beyond them turned stark white, as if all but the elevator flashed out of existence in the blink of an eye. I peered through the closing gap at the white expanse before the doors blocked it from view. It was one of those things where it happened so fast, I couldn't be sure it had happened at all. For all I knew, it was sunlight flashing in my eye, and my retina saw only white for a split second.

As the elevator rose, I felt warm breath on the back of my neck. I knew I'd entered the elevator alone. No one had been in it; I was sure of that. I turned to look behind me, and as expected, no one was there. Despite logic, those moments never fail to frighten even the most sensible adult. Children aren't the only ones with an instinctual fear of the supernatural. No matter what they say, adults have their own monsters under the bed.

I shuddered at the thought of mine.

The floor number display rose above three without stopping. *Damn it,* I thought. *Someone probably pressed it above, and for some reason it didn't drop me off first.* But the number went beyond five, up to six, and my heart pounded harder with each numerical increase. The building only had five floors.

The number finally stopped at eight. The doors opened.

I stared blankly at the long hallway outside the elevator. It appeared old, ruined, left to rot – the innards of a place uncared for, forgotten. "What the hell?" I said to myself. I jammed the button to go back down, but nothing happened. The doors stayed open, the elevator didn't move, the damn button wouldn't even light up. It seemed to have lost power, all except for that red number eight.

"Son of a bitch." I slammed my fist against the button panel. "Come on...please work!" I pressed the buttons haphazardly, hoping for a reaction, but still nothing.

I stepped out of the lift to see if anyone was around. "Hello? I think something's wrong with the elevator!"

I was met only by a cool breeze against my face. It carried the smell of filth. Human waste. Trash, piss, shit, vomit, all at once, as if combined in some kind of stew from Hell. I held my nose against it and tried not to gag, but I couldn't keep it out. It permeated my senses, causing my eyes to water and my gut to cramp. I managed to hold my resolve, barely, and stepped out of the elevator to find help. As confusing as the situation was, as surreal as it appeared, I knew I just had to find someone to get my bearings set straight.

"Hello?" I called out, making my way down the hall. The wet carpet squished beneath my feet. Although no lights worked, the hallway was still lit in a cold shade of blue. I had no idea where the illumination came from.

I looked into rooms off to the right and left, but they were all empty, furniture knocked on its side, papers strewn about. It looked like the remnants of an office building that had been deserted and never returned to. It looked like something bad had happened here... I tried not to think about how little sense the place made. It was a place that shouldn't have existed, yet here I was, right in it, a prisoner within its decaying walls.

A strong gust of air came in my direction, and as I approached the end there was the silhouette of movement behind a frosted-glass door. I reached for the knob, but hesitated before turning it. The howl of wind behind it, and the rapidly fluttering movements on the other side, made me question the decision. But I didn't have much choice. I opened it anyway.

All breath left me when I saw what was on the other side. The entire wall of the building was gone, open to the landscape of a crumbling city. Darkness reigned, not a flicker of light dancing anywhere on the stage of destruction I witnessed. Office buildings, houses, stores, they all remained in skeletal form – dead, but still decaying. I stood in one of them, looking out at the rest.

"I'm dreaming," I told myself. "This can't be real. It's a fucking nightmare."

The cityscape was bleak, barren of life. Clouded darkness hung over it. It was the end of days. It was the world I described to Barry in acute detail. Even the stench of the air was reminiscent of the stories I told my brother.

*It's gotta be a damn dream,* I told myself. *But it feels so real.*

The argument went back and forth in my head. Reality and illusion clashed, a battle of life and death. If this was truly the world, I was in for a bad time.

*Wake up, you dumb bastard. Just wake the fuck up already.* I wanted it to be over. I wanted to go back to the real world, where the apocalypse only existed within the bunker under my house. In Barry's mind it was real. It couldn't be real in mine. No fucking way.

The floor crumbled beneath my feet. My heart stopped as gravity took hold and pulled me down into the rubble eight stories down. The world spun with dizzying fury. Then all went black.

I awoke on my bed in the fallout shelter. Shuffling came from behind the door – the same horrible sound Barry made when he waddled around. I cringed, guilt crawling up my back. I wasn't a monster. I had a conscience, but I had to push that aside for Barry's sake.

The door opened, and there, moping in, was Barry.

"Barry? What's going on?"

"You took a nasty fall, brother. But you're okay now. We found you and got you home."

"You left the shelter?" My heart pounded harder than ever.

"What do you mean?" he asked, as if it were no big deal. As if it were normal.

"But–"

Before I could finish my sentence, a child entered the room. Strange that I felt relief at her appearance. As unusual as her presence there was, the end of the world certainly couldn't be true. Her dress was too clean, too new. I went to get up from the bed, but the girl put her palm up.

"Sit down, silly. You need to rest! We don't want you to hurt yourself."

I looked to my brother. "What the hell's going on, Barry?"

He smiled, if you could describe that hideous mouth doing such a thing. "Like I said, you fell and got hurt. Victoria and I helped you back home."

"That we did," the girl said, smiling brightly. She wagged a finger at me. "You should be thanking us rather than asking questions, mister."

"Who are you?" I asked. *Oh God*, I thought. *Barry somehow got out and brought some kid down here. Christ! I've gotta get this kid out of here.*

"Barry just told you who I am. I'm Victoria." She bobbed her head back and forth as she swayed side to side, hands wrapped behind her.

"Well, we'd better get you home, kid. Where do you live?"

She giggled at my inquiry. "The question is, where do *you* live?"

I looked hard at Barry. "Where'd you find this kid?"

"She was wandering the wasteland," he said. "We saved her, don't you remember?"

"He must have hit his head pretty badly," Victoria added. "It could have affected his memory."

"You think so?" Barry asked, concern wrinkling his already crumpled face.

"Could be," Victoria said. "He doesn't remember me."

"Do you remember me, brother?" Barry's eyes widened with hope.

"Of course I do," I answered as I stood. "There's nothing wrong with my memory. Come on, kid, we gotta get you home." I grabbed the girl by the arm and pulled her along toward the exit.

"No!" Barry screamed. "Don't go! It's dark out. Too dangerous!"

I opened the hatch and unlocked the upper exit. As I went upstairs, girl in tow, Barry ran to the bottom and hollered up at me.

"Please! Just come back," Barry pleaded. "I don't want you to die."

"I'm not going to die, Barry. This kid doesn't belong here. There isn't enough food." I tried to perpetuate the lie, even though I was sure Barry had gone outside. I retained some hope that he hadn't gone far, and just didn't know the difference between the real world and the illusion I'd put in his brain. "We'll starve if she stays." I said it as if I believed it myself.

"She won't," Barry said. "She can help us."

"No, Barry, she can't. And we can't help her."

I left Barry behind me, didn't even bother to lock the door. What the fuck did it matter at this point? But when I got to the top of the stairs I stopped dead. My legs buckled and I fell to my knees. The house was nothing more than some splinters of rotten wood. The entire neighborhood was a faded memory of its former self. Everything was as I'd described to Barry. The lie was all around me, physical, real: I could even smell death in the air.

Victoria circled me and faced me with her arms crossed. "He told you not to come out here."

*Have I lost it? Is it possible to lie so long it becomes real?*

"Anything is possible," the girl said in a stern voice.

*What the hell? Did she read my mind?*

She giggled, an unnatural sound. "No, silly. You're thinking out loud, is all."

I tried to stand, to demand to be told what was happening. But my legs didn't have the strength, and my voice lacked the will. My soul had lost its rigid outer layer. I was vulnerable to my surroundings. I wasn't in control.

"I'd tell you to stay calm," Victoria said, "but it wouldn't do any good."

A thunderous sound came toward us. My lungs stopped taking in air, blood halted in my veins, synapses in my brain momentarily ceased to fire; when I looked toward the terror-inducing sound, a grotesque titan of a thing approached. It pounded along the long-decayed remnants of the street on giant legs. It looked like Barry. That was the worst part. It looked so much like him, but enormous, and even further malformed.

"What the fuck is that?" I asked the girl.

"That's what lives in your world. In Barry's world. They rule his dreams. He sees you as a hero. The only one who can fight them off and protect him. Good luck."

Before I could say anything, she was no longer there. Vanished. Gone.

But the giant nightmare lumbering in my direction was as real as anything.

I forced my legs to work with everything I had, and got myself upright. I managed to get one foot in front of the other, forming some kind of drunken-looking gait. My legs felt as though they'd snap under the crushing weight of fear. They had no strength. They hobbled along at barely a jog. I was afraid to look behind me and see how close death was, but I figured it was better not to know.

As the ground beneath my feet rumbled less and less, and my lungs could no longer get enough air to keep me going, I collapsed like a sack of boneless flesh. I thought if death were to come, I might as well get it over with.

*To hell with it. If this really is the world, what's the point of living anyway?*

"I wonder if that's how your brother feels."

I shot up at the girl's voice. She stood next to me, staring at me with eyes that seemed to glow.

"What?" It appeared to be the only word I could come up with.

"What's he got to live for if this is the world?"

"But it's not–"

"Oh, but it is." She put her hands on her hips. "To Barry this is all real. And now, it's real for you too."

She kicked dirt in my face. By the time I rubbed it out of my eyes, she was already gone. I was again alone in that dreary, dead world of Barry's imagination.

But was it really his imagination? Was it mine? Was it real? I couldn't be sure of anything anymore. The only thing I clung to was that girl who didn't belong here. She didn't fit. There was something odd about her. She was too normal for the world I saw around me, but too unusual for the world as I knew it before.

I struggled to my feet, wobbly but upright. I spat ashy dust, tried to moisten my dried mouth, but there didn't seem to be any saliva left. The air permeated me both inside and out. Its wretched stink seeped in; I felt as though it would never come out, and the taste on my tongue would last forever.

Just as I thought I should go back to the bunker, try to get some answers from Barry, maybe find that girl and get some answers from her, a heavy wind kicked up. Ashen filth from the ground filled the air, creating a fog of black and gray. I couldn't tell which direction I'd come from. I didn't know which way led back home. Even in my own neighborhood, I was lost. With everything I knew destroyed, I had no bearing on my location.

I was lost.

Panic shook my hands. I tightened them into fists in an attempt to steady them, but the tremors only went up my arms and into my jaw. I shook as though standing in the snow naked. But my skin didn't feel cold; it burned with fear.

For the first time in my life, all I wanted was to see was Barry's face. That horrid, deformed insult to humanity had become the only beacon of hope I could reach for.

It seemed so far away. But I knew I couldn't have gone *that* far in the short distance my legs had been able to carry me away from that horrid monster. I couldn't be much farther than down the street. But wherever home was, in the impenetrable fog it seemed like forever away.

I tried to pinpoint where I was by my surroundings, tried to put the crumbled houses back together in my head like puzzles with scattered pieces, but there wasn't enough to go on. Most of the parts were missing, the puzzles incomplete. The rotten wood stakes sticking up from the eroded foundations were nothing more than gravestones in memory of a dead world.

With no other option available, I chose the direction I thought might be the way, and began walking. The dark wind storm blew the dust of a lost world in my eyes, in my nose, right down my throat. I covered my mouth with my arm, but the bitter taste of my own filthy clothing made me gag. Despite the raging nausea and aches in my legs, I continued on, like some despairing soldier returning home on foot from a lost war.

The wind struck harder, lashed at my face with cruelty. I barred my teeth against it and sealed my lips to keep out the dust. But no matter what I did, it seemed to penetrate every part of me, inside and out. My eyes stung, too dry to even water the dirt from their surfaces. My lungs sucked in short breaths of toxic air. I thought I would die out here, that the thoughts in my head would be my last. There would be no one to bury me. My body would either be picked clean by scavengers, if any survived out here, or be left to decay alone.

I tried to shake those thoughts; the despair would have been enough to carry me to death. But the loneliness of their nature burned behind my retinas. Within swirls of dirt-filled air, I saw my own corpse. I stopped in horror at the sight of myself. I looked fresh. Couldn't have been there long. I wondered if I were already dead, nothing more than non-corporeal remnants of what I used to be, or if dehydration and fear had brought on madness. I held both hands out in front of me, turned them over. I patted myself down. I felt real. But would I even know the difference if I were dead?

I nudged my own corpse with my shoe. My limp body rolled over, eyes stuck open, eyes that would never see again. The sight brought acidic bile to the top of my throat, but I held it down, swallowed hard against the sickness in my gut.

I wanted to think it was all an elaborate dream, but the suffering was too intense. Whatever was happening, no matter how insane, was absolutely real. But even with that knowledge, I knew something wasn't quite right. Something was off about the whole thing.

Just then something broke through the screaming wind. A soft tune, lullaby notes: far off, but distinguishable. I followed the music, determined to discover its source, and hopefully my salvation.

"Hello!" I called out, trying to raise my voice above the howling wind. "Listen up, little girl! I know you have something to do with this. Where the hell are you?"

Her voice came from right behind me. "I'm right here, silly."

I lost my breath in surprise as I turned to see her standing not more than two feet away, wearing a big smile on her face. She held a music box in her hands that glowed with a strange green luminescence – the source of the music.

"I've been with you the whole time," she said. "And you're going the wrong way, just so you know."

"Just tell me what's going on." I dropped to my knees. "Please...I'm begging."

Victoria looked up, and she placed her pointer finger against her chin as she thought about it. "No," she said. "I don't think I want to. Besides, your brother is out here looking for you. You might want to go find him first."

"Oh no," I cried. "He'll never last out here alone."

She laughed cruelly at my words. "Doesn't seem like you're faring too well either."

"Please," I begged, "just tell me where he is!"

She pointed to my left. "He went that way."

I struggled to my feet and tried to run, but only managed to hobble. Still, it was faster than the slow shamble I'd paced before. I regretfully took large breaths to keep myself going. The acrid taste of death coated my throat. Involuntary coughing failed to remove it.

A silhouette in the near-zero visibility caught my attention. It looked like Barry. It didn't have the body of a normal human being; its shape, although hard to see, was comparable to his.

"Barry! Are you okay?"

It turned around, and when I saw its mangled face – horrifically more distorted than Barry's hideous visage – my gut sank. "Oh, fuck."

It responded with a wet growl and came at me, mouth open, drool running down its lower half. It wrapped its thin arms around my leg and bit into my thigh. A dry howl of pain left my throat and disappeared into the wind. I fell on my back as I kicked, trying to get the miserable wretch off me. Its jaws only closed harder, deeper into fat and muscle. Blood oozed from the wound, quickly turning black as it soaked in ash from the air.

I writhed on the ground, pounding against the vicious thing's head with both fists, but it didn't seem to be concerned with my attack. Either it was too strong for me to hurt it, or it was so ravenously hungry it didn't care about anything other than feeding.

Out of energy and willpower, I allowed myself to fall limp on my back. The pain reached a threshold of shock, my mind numbed by it. *Just let go... There's nothing you can do anyway.*

A loud bang sounded off. At the same time, thick blood sprayed over my face. The pressure on my leg released, and the filthy thing dropped dead. Barry's disgusting head loomed over me.

"I'm so glad I found you!" he said. "I thought you'd be lost forever." He embraced me with his spindly arms. He gasped when he saw my leg. "Oh no! You're hurt! We've gotta get you home. Come on, Victoria, help me carry him."

The little girl stepped beside me with a smug look on her face. They lifted me off the ground. I had trouble believing she had that much strength – she or Barry, for that matter. But as consciousness drifted further away, I cared less about how they were able to carry me.

The last thing I heard before passing out was the girl's voice whispering, "All you have to do is open the door."

*   *   *

When I woke, Barry was standing over me with that large, misshapen, watchful eye. I sat upright. "Where's that girl?" I asked.

"She's not here."

"Where the hell did she go?"

He only shrugged.

I tried to stand, but fell back onto the bed. My leg was wrapped in old cloth, soaked red.

"Sit down, brother. You need to rest that leg."

"No, I need to talk to the girl. What's her name?"

"Victoria."

"Well, get her in here."

"I told you, she's not here." He turned to leave the room. "I'll go get you some water. You probably need it."

When he closed the door, Victoria's laugh echoed in the tiny makeshift bedroom. The steel walls added a metallic, un-human characteristic to the sound that scraped my eardrums.

"Do you remember what I said?"

I looked over, and there she was. Somehow she'd been in the room the whole time.

Anger left me. Finally facing her, I felt more desperation than rage. "Please, just tell me what's going on. I'm so confused."

"I can't explain what's happening. But you need to open the door."

"I don't understand."

Her brow crinkled, eyes staring hard. "I think you do."

Her stare penetrated my mind, and suddenly I began to see. "Do you really think he'll fare better out there? Isn't it safer for him down here?"

"Open the door. Or don't."

"I never wanted to lie to him…" As my words trailed off, she was gone. Yet again she'd vanished, leaving me to solve whatever puzzle was ahead. But the answer was clear. I had a choice to make.

I forced myself to stand against the pain in my leg. I left the room, looked at Barry. Something about me must have said something to him, because his expression changed, a face of his I'd never seen before. For some reason, it didn't look so hideous anymore, just different. I went to the vault door, opened it, and unlocked the secondary door. As I ascended the basement stairs, I left them open behind me.

It was Barry's time to choose.

The Ninth Story: Fear / Doubt

# Escape
# by K. B. Goddard

John Merryweather walked with slow steps homeward. It was a fine night. Stars shone bright and lustrous in a clear, cloudless sky; not to be outdone, the full orb of the moon had ascended in its blue-white raiment to preside over the night sky. The air was sweet and fresh, the night warm. There came only the gentle soughing of the wind and the cry of a night bird to break in upon the silence.

Yet John walked on, oblivious to the charms of the evening. His mind was elsewhere. As an artist, such a night would once have invoked a sense of rapture and driven him to his sketchbook. Now, though, his thoughts lay in another direction.

All week long he had suffered from disturbed sleep and uncomfortable dreams. His dreams, however, only grew from the occupations and fears of his waking mind.

When he reached home, he hung up his hat behind the door and crossed to a chair, ignoring the unfinished work on the easel, half-buried amid a confusion of paints and brushes, canvases and paper. He dropped down into the chair and flung his head back. It could not go on like this, really it could not. He badly needed a distraction. He could not work, for his mind continually wandered back to his dilemma. He picked up the book he had been reading from the table next to his chair, where he had discarded it the night before, and set himself to try to read a few pages as a preliminary to bed. In this endeavour, he was not wholly unsuccessful.

A while later, he closed his book and looked at the clock on the mantle; it was almost a quarter past eleven. He yawned and stretched himself out; his fatigued body was urging him toward bed. Tired though he was, he did not relish the notion of sleep, for sleep would only bring the return of the dreams that haunted him. The lonely silence of his rooms echoed within him.

He sighed, lighted his candle, and put out the lamps. Passing between the shifting shadows thrown by his candle, he crossed the sitting-room towards the door that communicated with his bedroom. The clock was chiming the quarter hour as he laid his hand upon the doorknob.

He froze for a moment. Surely that was a noise from within the room. Could someone have gained entry? Impossible. In any case, he had little enough that would reward a burglar's efforts. It was imagination only. He was tired, and his senses were playing tricks on him.

He threw wide the door and saw within the room...nothing. Nothing, that is, save for his usual furnishings. He stepped into the room. There was no one there. Of course there was not, and yet it was not the first time he'd had the feeling of not being alone in his rooms. Lately, he'd more than once had the feeling he was being watched. He pushed the feeling aside as best he could, closed the door behind him, and went to bed.

In his sleep, his features slipped into a progressively deeper frown. His face bore an oddly melancholic expression. The colour rose in his cheeks, and his lips gave shape to a word that looked like 'Alice'.

Morning broke, the daylight bringing the slow, giddy relinquishment of sleep. John raised his head from the pillow, bleary-eyed and blinking. The sensation of being watched, which had been so insistent the night before, had somewhat abated. It was never as strong during the hours of daylight.

As the fog of sleep cleared, he became aware that the light was flickering. This made no sense; it was daylight now, and daylight did not flicker. It was a moment before his mind cleared enough for him to realise where the flickering light was coming from. The door was open about an inch, and a red light was emanating through the gap. His first thought was one of confusion. He had, he knew, closed the door when he went to bed. His second thought was one of concern. Was there a fire?

He jumped from the bed and ran to the door. As he laid his hand on the panels, he observed that the door was not hot; neither was there a smell of smoke to indicate a fire. He stood irresolutely for a moment, his brows creased. He was uncertain, and he did not like uncertainty. He pulled open the door and stepped through.

It has been previously stated that the door to his bedroom communicated with the sitting-room; it was not, however, his sitting-room in which John found himself. Instead, he was now standing in what appeared to be the foyer of a large building, perhaps a hotel.

A layer of fine dust lay over the floor and the desk. Cobwebs created an intricate seal over the openings of the disused pigeon-holes behind the desk. It appeared that no post had troubled their gossamer curtains for some time.

The red light continued to flash somewhere overhead, but the source was not clear. He could see no gas jets or candles, nothing to account for the light. It was as though the air itself were flashing red, pulsing with fiery energy.

From the gloom beyond, there came a mechanical clunking and whirring. Barely did he have time to wonder at what was happening to him before he was startled anew by the sudden sound of a disembodied voice coming to him out of the ether:

'Emergency! Emergency! We have had an escape from floor nine! Please proceed to the lift.'

This was curious enough, but still more curious was the fact that the voice seemed to be that of a child, a little girl. The voice came again.

'Emergency! Please take the lift to floor nine. John Merryweather to floor nine.'

John froze. Whoever the voice belonged to, they knew who he was. Clearly he was expected. But just where was he? In front of him, a door slid open to reveal a lift. By some strange compulsion, he walked forward and peered inside. A moment later he was sprawled on the floor of the lift as an unseen force pulled him into the interior. He scrambled to his feet and brushed himself off in as dignified a manner as he could manage in the circumstances.

'Sorry,' came the voice, from beside him this time. He leapt back as he realised that a little girl with blonde curls was standing beside him; she was holding a music box and peeping up at him with an apologetic expression. How did she...? She wasn't there a moment ago.

'Who...?' he managed to say.

'Sorry,' said the child again. 'My name is Victoria Bigglesworth-Hayes. I did not mean to startle you, but I need your help.'

'My help? Where am I, anyway?'

'Usually this is a lost place. So many lost things are here, and I am one of them.' She sighed and looked down at her boots. 'But now I've *misplaced* one of the lost things, and I need your help to get it back. I'm quite new to this, you see.'

'Child, you talk in riddles. You are making no sense.'

'I'll do my best to explain everything in a moment.' Then, as though she was speaking to the air, she suddenly called out, 'Floor nine, please.' The mechanical whirring came again as the lift creaked into life. John clung to the tarnished gilt walls of the lift in terror.

'What is happening?' he cried.

'We are going to floor nine.'

'How did you...?'

'Probably best not to ask.' She looked down at the music box in her hands and patted it fondly. 'Do you like my music box?' she asked. He stared at her blankly. 'Perhaps you'd like it to play you a tune; you seem a little discomposed,' she said, tilting her head to the side and blinking up at him innocently.

She turned the crank on the side of the box; it began to play a soft, haunting melody that seemed to seep into his soul and soothe him. He found that he no longer questioned anything that was happening to him as strange; he felt as though he were merely lost inside a daydream.

There was a slight jolt as the lift stopped. The door slid back on its own, and he saw a gas-lit corridor beyond.

'Floor nine,' declared the girl. 'Follow me.' He did so without question, trailing along behind like an obedient child. She walked along the passage until she came to a set of large double doors; these she pushed open, and beckoned him inside.

He found himself in a library of colossal proportions. Books everywhere; books as far as the eye could see. Before him was a table that had apparently been freshly laid for tea.

'Do sit down,' said Victoria. 'I need to speak with you about something, and it might be difficult to explain. We have work to do, but you are clearly not in a state to go anywhere yet. This place can be quite disorientating. I'm sure you will feel better after some tea.'

'It's breakfast time.'

'Is it? Time doesn't really mean much here.' She shrugged. 'I thought we would have tea in here. It's quite my favourite room. I love books. I love stories.'

'Do you?' asked John, as she poured a cup of tea from a pink china teapot and handed it to him.

'Oh, yes,' she replied. 'Sandwich?'

'Thank you,' he said.

'Yes, I love stories. Would you like me to tell you one?'

'All right.'

'But you mustn't interrupt,' she said in a manner somewhat reminiscent of a nanny to her charge.

'I promise,' he replied meekly.

'Once there was a little girl who found herself all alone in the world, without any mother or father, all alone in a lost place. Alone, that is, apart from the creatures that lived in the darkness. Sometimes visitors would come and see the girl when they needed to make a choice, and she would guide them on their way. Sometimes, if they made the wrong choice, they never left. But they didn't really find her; the lost place found them. Then one day something escaped from the lost place, and the girl needed the help of a brave hero to bring it back. And that is where you come in, Mr Merryweather.'

'I?'

Yes, you. You see, the thing that has escaped is in your home.'

'I don't quite follow.'

'Have some more tea,' she said, refilling his cup. 'Cake?' She offered him a plate, and he picked up a slice of cake without ever stopping to think how peculiar all of this was.

'Thank you.'

'The thing that escaped,' she continued, 'it belongs in this place. It was never meant for your world; its powers will be far stronger outside of the confines of this place. There is too much to feed on out there.'

'What do you mean, "feed on?"'

'The human mind.'

What was he to make of that? He didn't know who this strange child was, but she did not talk like any child he'd ever known. This was all too much for his comprehension.

'Good heavens!' he declared. 'Are you suggesting there is some wild creature in my rooms that... that... eats brains?'

'Ewww. No, of course not.' She wrinkled her nose in disgust, and frowned for a moment, as if in thought. 'Although there might be one of those on the second floor,' she said as she gazed absently into the distance. She shook her head. 'No, I mean the mind, the thoughts, the personality, not the physical brain.'

'But what you are saying is fantastic.'

'There are more things in heaven and earth...'

'How then am I to be rid of it?'

'That is rather awkward; you must defeat it.'

'I? Defeat it?' John had a vision of himself in bare-handed combat with some wild creature. It was not a favourable image.

'Yes. You see, it has attached itself to you. So you must be the one to defeat it.'

'I?' he asked again. 'But how?'

'You must break the link between you.'

'But if we are connected, should it not already be back here?' he asked.

Victoria shook her head. 'It won't come back voluntarily. Even if you can stay here long enough to weaken your link to it, it will just attach itself to someone else. The only way to defeat it is for you to conquer it.' She rose suddenly. 'We must go now, before it gets any stronger. Come.' She beckoned him to follow her.

He put down his teacup and rose to go with her. As she led him out of the door and back towards the lift, he asked, 'If it does not need to be where I am, why is it still in my rooms?'

'A fair question,' she conceded. She quickened her pace slightly, and he found himself once more before the lift doors. 'It is in a strange world, and it has already found its prey. It will build its strength from you, and then there's no telling what it might do.' There came the sound of sliding metal as the lift doors opened.

She stepped inside the lift, and he followed. He was utterly bewildered. He could only conclude that he was subject to a bizarre dream. As he did not show signs of waking, it seemed the best course was to simply follow where his guide led him. If nothing else, he would come out of this with inspiration enough for several paintings.

When the doors opened again, they stepped out into near-total darkness. Although they could see each other perfectly well, they seemed to be surrounded by thick, swirling black fog, thicker than any pea-souper; it crawled about them with an oily slickness. What lay beyond the fog was impossible to see. Yet there was the impression of movement, shadows in the fog.

'Where are we? I wish you wouldn't keep doing that; it's so disconcerting.'

'We are supposed to be in your rooms. This was not me. It must be the Doubt.'

'The doubt?' he asked, squinting through the fog.

Victoria nodded. 'Yes, a distant cousin of the nightmare.'

'The...'

'Yes,' she said, not waiting for him to finish, 'and like the nightmare, they can also create dreams. Unlike the nightmare, they prey solely on the fear that comes from doubt. All those choices we struggle to make for fear of the outcome, the questioning of our own worth and ability, all the natural doubts of humanity used as a weapon against it. You have them here too, but the ones from the lost place are far more powerful. Once they get inside your mind, they turn every doubt you hold against you. Even the smallest

215

anxiety will become intolerably painful.'

'None of this makes sense. I...' He broke off suddenly and assumed a listening attitude.

Through the dense fog echoed the sound of footsteps. The steps drew nearer. Victoria and John drew closer together. From the swirling vapours, two figures emerged.

Two young women strolled into view. At first, the parasols they were carrying concealed their faces, but as they turned their heads, John started. One was dark and the other fair, but it was upon the dark one that John's eyes were fixed.

Victoria's gaze passed from her companion to the vision and back again. A green light seemed to shine behind the eyes of the unearthly child, but John hardly noticed; he saw only the dark-haired vision before him.

'Alice,' he whispered.

The figures were beginning to speak.

'He proposed to you?' asked the fair-haired girl.

'Yes! Can you imagine?' replied Alice.

'Surely he did not actually expect you to accept him.'

'I cannot imagine what he was thinking,' said Alice scornfully.

'You, marry an artist? The very idea.' The fair-haired girl looked shocked.

'It was something of a liberty. As though I could ever think of marrying so far beneath myself.' Alice's tones conveyed a sense of distaste, and perhaps just a hint of pity.

John's gaze fell to the ground. Victoria crossed her arms in front of her, her jaw set firmly.

'You have always been very kind to him, of course,' said the fair-haired young lady.

'My dear Martha, I am kind to everyone. Besides, he was painting my likeness. It would not have done to be unkind; he might not have sufficiently flattered me.' They laughed, the pleasant musical tone of their laughter giving way to harsh derisive cackles. Their mocking voices echoed all around, swirling and twisting about them like tendrils of the fog as the figures were absorbed back into the darkness.

John clamped his hands over his ears; the wretched sound tore through his mind, shredding his nerves. He felt a tight grip take his arm. Victoria's voice chimed out as the laughter faded away.

'Listen to me. It is not real. It is using your own fears against you.'

'But it may be true.'

'That is what doubt does, but the possibilities it shows you are only one side of the coin.'

There was a rushing sensation in the air about them. The fog parted to reveal an object. As the fog continued to roll back, the object became clearer; it was an armchair upholstered in red velvet. Seated in the chair was a stately-looking elderly woman; before her stood a facsimile of John himself, head bowed in subjugation. The old woman sat enthroned in her chair, glaring straight at John's double, her face set rigid, her eyes blazing.

'You wish to marry my granddaughter!' she

shrieked. 'How dare you? I will not countenance such an outrage. This is how you repay me for my hospitality? You presume to...'

'I love her,' came the reply of the second John.

'Love? Love! You talk to me of love? Fool! Do you think a young lady of her advantages could ever condescend to love the likes of you, a penniless artist? You embarrass yourself by your folly, sir. What of love? Even if she were foolish enough to love you, what then? You can offer her nothing. She has a position to maintain. No, sir, you shall never marry her. Never!'

That last word echoed through the fog as the vision faded.

'No more, no more. I cannot endure it.'

'You have to fight it. Try to picture the other side.'

But another vision was already forming. This time, two gentlemen stood before a painting.

'Abominable,' said one.

'The perspective is all wrong,' said the other, scowling.

'The composition does not help.'

'I cannot say that I see much to recommend it, but then I find all his paintings to be rather indifferent.'

'A very indifferent artist altogether. It isn't even bad enough to be interesting.'

'Honestly, I cannot see why Anstruther ever agreed to exhibit him.'

'I believe he knew his father. It must have been on account of their friendship. He could never have got in here on his own merit.'

'I hear he hopes to marry.'

'Marry? I cannot see how he can hope to support a wife through his art if this is the best he can do.'

'Don't listen!' Victoria's voice broke in upon the scene. How distant it seemed to John in his tortured state. He continued staring ahead of him, at the two figures dissecting his work. She took John by the arms and shook him until he turned away. He shook his head as the fog rolled back in, swallowing the two gentlemen.

'Fight it!'

'How?' he muttered hopelessly.

'Look at me. Look at me!'

He turned to face her. Her eyes...so green, luminous, like a cat's in the dark. 'You have to see the other side,' she continued. 'Picture to yourself the alternative. What if she says yes? What if you do become a great artist?'

'What if she says no? What if my art is never appreciated?'

'What then? Can the reality of that be any worse than what you've already experienced a thousand times in your mind?'

He shook his head.

'You've already seen the worst, so why not let yourself see the best possible outcome?' asked Victoria. 'Close your eyes and imagine it. See yourself propose. See her say yes. See yourself succeed.'

He closed his eyes, his features contorted with

the effort of thought.

'I can't,' he cried. 'It won't let me.' He gasped for breath, the strain pulling his mind asunder.

'Try!'

He tried to clear his mind of the negative thoughts that crowded in upon it. It was as though the fog were now inside his mind, carrying with it the fuel to the burning fire of his thoughts. He forced himself to focus. He pushed aside the visions, picturing Alice as he knew her, smiling and sweet. He tried to imagine the joy he would feel if she accepted him.

'I think it's working,' he heard Victoria say. 'Keep going. Picture your wedding; see it in your mind.'

He did as he was bid, as best as he could. It took all his inner resolve not to focus on what seemed his likely rejection.

Gradually, he felt the fog receding.

'It's working!' cried Victoria. 'Keep going. I will try to bind it.' He heard a small clicking sound beside him, and music began to play. The girl must be using the music box. He kept his eyes closed tightly and made himself concentrate. It was easier now than before; he knew the fog's influence over him had weakened.

As the music played beside him, he heard another sound: a deep, guttural roar of anger. Involuntarily, he opened his eyes.

They were in his rooms. The remaining fog was now in one corner of his sitting room. There was something odd about it, something alive.

It seemed to be shaping itself into some solid form. In a moment, it became clear. Before them stood a fearsome and powerful beast in the guise of a horse.

Victoria continued to turn the crank of the music box. The creature writhed and riled, as though it sought to free itself of some invisible restraint. The monstrous muscles rippled as the great beast reared up, snorting hot breath through flared nostrils. In the eyes, a fire like two burning coals blazed hot and red with rage.

John's legs felt weak as he looked upon the monstrous spectacle. His heart tightened in his chest, the sharp thrill of fear coursed through his blood. He wanted to run, more than anything. His fear had given strength to this monster. How was he to contend with such a creature?

That moment of doubt was all it took. The beast whinnied and reared up with such ferocity that Victoria went flying in her attempts to get out from under its flailing hooves. There was an audible metallic snapping sound, as of chains breaking. A moment later, it was free; the horse bolted, smashing through the sitting-room door in its egress.

'Quick, after it,' Victoria shouted.

They were running down the stairs into the hall. The hall door had been rent from its hinges.

'I hope my landlady is not home. How am I going to explain this?'

'Not now, John.'

They ran through the open doorway and out into the street. Only now did he realise that it was night. It was morning when his adventure had begun; how could it be night-time already?

They looked up and down the road, just in time to see by the light from the street lamps the dark figure of the horse disappearing around the corner.

'What now?' asked John. 'We will never catch it on foot.'

'In here.' Victoria ran up to a brougham that was parked opposite the house and pulled the door open. 'Get in.'

'But...'

'Get in!' The brougham was not unattended, as John had at first thought. A figure in a dark cloak and a top hat was perched on the driver's box. John could not make out the face, but the figure inclined his head toward Victoria.

'Follow that horse, William,' she cried. The driver nodded as they scrambled into the carriage.

'You know the driver?' he asked as the horses darted off.

'Yes. It's a long story, but I was afraid we might need him tonight.'

'Tonight, yes, why is it night? I left in the morning.'

'I'm not exactly sure. Time works strangely in the lost place. I think having something escape may have distorted time somehow, as though a bit of the lost place's time structure has leaked out with it. Which is bad news for us, because the Doubt is stronger at night.'

'Wonderful.'

The carriage rattled on through the darkness. They travelled swiftly, the street lamps passing in quick succession. Victoria squinted through the windows for any sign of the feral creature. After a few minutes, the carriage pulled up sharply, with protesting cries from the horses. The occupants were flung forward. They picked themselves up and leapt out of the carriage. The brougham had pulled up in front of a dead end. The driver raised a hand to indicate the alley. Victoria nodded.

They edged forwards into the opening of the alley. It took time for John's eyes to adjust to the gloom. Victoria's eyes seemed to shine with a strange light of their own. They searched the darkness.

'Why does it not simply turn back into fog?' he asked in a whisper.

'Kindly do not give it any ideas. Besides, it cannot; we've weakened it enough that it is stuck in physical form. Now you need to complete the task.'

They saw it then, two spots of burning red against the blackness that shrouded the far end of the alley. Then it was coming for them, fire blazing in its eyes and smoke billowing from the flaring nostrils as it came into the light.

They dived aside, narrowly avoiding being ground into the cobbles by the raging hooves. The beast stopped short of ploughing into the waiting brougham. The carriage horses reared in terror and strained to escape the devilish mirror of their own form. The driver fought to keep them from bolting.

The beast was turning. Now they were trapped

in the alley. They backed away. They could not go very far, though, without being lost in the darkness. John looked around for a means of escape, a gate or a garden wall that they could climb. In the meagre light from the carriage lamps and the street lamp that stood sentinel at the entrance to the alley, they watched the great beast preparing to charge again.

'You have to stop it!' cried Victoria. 'When it charges, you must defy it. Face your fears, or it will kill you.'

'Excellent.'

But something else was stirring in the shadows. The beast had seen it too, and was momentarily distracted. It stamped its hooves. It looked as though it was trying to crush something. Then they saw what the second shape was.

Weaving itself back and forth around the legs of the horse was a cat! A little kitten emerged from beneath the horse with the unconcerned air inherent in the feline population. As the monster reared up again, threatening to land a devastating blow, the kitten hopped nimbly aside and looked on with an air of no more than casual interest.

Despite the horror of his situation, John smiled. If such a tiny creature could toy with this terror, then surely he could find valour enough to defy it.

The beast was scraping its hoof against the cobbles. They backed away another step. A split second later, it was coming for them. It was almost upon them when John closed his eyes, inhaled, and thought of Alice.

He waited, but the blow never came. Squinting, he opened one eye, then the other. There was no sign of the horse.

'You did it!' shouted Victoria.

'Where did it go?'

'I have bound it. It will return to the lost place now.' She was holding her music box before her. He could swear he saw it rattle in her hands. He did not press the point; he had a feeling that the explanation would only give him a headache.

They walked back to the brougham, the little grey kitten keeping pace with them. As John opened the door, the kitten hopped in and sat on the seat. Victoria laughed.

'I think she wants to come with us. She's lost, too.'

'How do you know?'

'I know lots of things,' came the enigmatic answer.

The cat remained curled up in Victoria's lap, purring contentedly, as the carriage rattled on its return journey. Now that the battle was won, John took the opportunity to question the girl.

'Why was that thing in the building in the first place?'

'People come to the lost place when they have choices to make. The Doubt is from floor nine; that's where people like you come to face their inner fears. It's usually more controlled than this, but out here in your world, it's far more dangerous.'

'Even now I don't believe it.'

The carriage drew up in front of his rooms, and John got out.

'Good luck, John Merryweather,' said Victoria.

'And to you, Miss.' They smiled at each other for a moment; then he closed the carriage door and walked up to his door. As he turned to take one last look, he started in surprise. Carriage, child, and cat were all gone, though he had heard no clatter of hooves, and no sign was there of the vehicle anywhere along the length of the street. He shook his head. It was just one more event in a night full of the inexplicable.

He was afraid to see what condition the hall door would be in, let alone that to his room, but he was astounded to see that there were no signs anywhere of the disturbance. He decided there was no point in questioning this either, and simply shrugged.

When he was back once more in his rooms, he crossed to the fire and took from the mantle a card. It read:

*You are invited to an exhibition of artworks by John Merryweather. The exhibition will take place on Saturday 4ᵗʰ October 1902 at Anstruther's Gallery.*

He read the words and smiled. Somewhere in his soul, he felt a flicker of hope.

He stood once more before the old lady. Mrs Montague was seated, as in his vision, in her accustomed armchair. She motioned for him to sit down. Her face was far less intimidating than in his vision. She looked at him appraisingly for a minute; finally, she spoke.

'You wish to marry my granddaughter?'

'Yes, ma'am, if she will have me.'

'I shall speak frankly, though it may be considered vulgar to do so. As you are aware, it is generally considered prudent to choose a spouse with at least some measure of consideration to material matters. There are good reasons for this, though often this means the same families intermarrying generation after generation, resulting in a very dull circle of people with no understanding of anything beyond their immediate social sphere.' She shook her head and recalled herself to the matter at hand. 'That said,' she continued, 'I have also seen many a maid marry a man worse off than herself merely because he had a title. Titles, wealth, and society, however, are no guarantee of happiness in a marriage. Love is no guarantee of happiness either, but I believe a marriage that has, or comes to have, love is more likely to be happy than one weighed entirely in the bank balance.

'I have said I shall be frank, and I shall. I should like you to be likewise, Mr Merryweather. Answer me truly: do you wish to marry Alice for material reasons, or for love?'

'For love!' he said without a moment's hesitation. She looked at him again with those keen eyes that saw all, still sharp despite their years, or perhaps because of them. Then the lines of her face broke into a smile.

'I believe you.' He sighed a sigh of relief. He had

evidently passed that particular test. 'Do you see that portrait?' said she, indicating a painting of a noble-looking young woman, which adorned a wall at the far end of the room.

'It is fine work. The lady is very handsome.'

'Yes, she was. That young lady is my dear mother in her youth. But do you know who painted it?'

'I do not recognise the hand.'

'It was painted by my father.' John raised his eyebrows, the very picture of astonishment, at which the old lady burst into a pleasant laugh, her old face creasing up with mirth. Her laugh reminded him very much of Alice's. He could not help smiling. 'I thought that might surprise you,' said she. 'Ah yes, my father, he was an artist, very much like you. He did not have very much, but oh, how he did love my mother. She had lost both her parents by the time she met him, and she was of age when he proposed. She had no one then to prevent her making a *bad marriage*; if she had, her life might have been very different, but as it was, they were one of the happiest couples I have ever known.'

'I had not the least idea.'

'That is one of the reasons that I make it a point to offer my help and patronage to young artists whenever I can. It is my way of honouring my late father. So yes, Mr Merryweather, I do give you my consent. If Alice will have you, you may marry her with all my best wishes for your future happiness.'

'I cannot tell you how happy you have made me.'

The old lady smiled kindly and said, 'She has

not said yes yet, Mr Merryweather; you must save some of your joy, you know. Ring that bell over there, if you would, and ask Jenkins to send for Alice.' He did as he was bid; a minute later Alice entered the room, the scent of wild roses drifting on the air around her.

After a few words, Mrs Montague made her exit and left the two young people alone. Alice looked up at him smiling. Her dark eyes drew him to her like an enchantment. He stepped closer to her. He heard her intake of breath.

'Alice,' said he, 'I am not a rich man, but if you will consent to marry me, I will work night and day to be worthy of you in all other ways.' Alice took his hand and held it tenderly, her smile broadening.

'I thought you'd never find the courage to ask!'

Theirs was a summer wedding. As they came out of the church as man and wife, the sun cast its smiling rays upon the happy couple as though in blessing of the union. Bees flew busily in the lavender beyond the church gates, and the wedding bells pealed in cheerful recognition of the happy day.

As he helped his new bride into the wedding carriage, John looked back into the crowd of friends and family. He could have sworn that, just for an instant, he had caught a glimpse of a fair-haired girl holding a fluffy grey cat. He stood smiling for a moment before his bride recalled his attention. He climbed into the carriage, and the happy couple drove away to embark upon their new life together without a doubt in their hearts.

# EXTRAS

# Music from
# The Lift Audio Drama

Victoria's Music Box is such an important part of our show, a powerful object, Victoria's constant companion and an important character in its own right.

Because of this, the music for the show's themes needed to be voiced by the music box, and have just the right mix of mystery, sadness, loss, and hope – not an easy task.

Luckily for us, we were able to partner with two very talented companies, Henninger-Parke Music, and We Talk of Dreams to create the perfect music.

Sean Parke and Kimberly Henninger created our opening theme and Nico Vettese of We Talk of Dreams wrote our closing theme and provides custom scoring for the lion share of our episodes.

# Victoria's Lift
### (The Lift opening theme)

Henninger Parke Music

# Victoria's Theme

We Talk of Dreams

# The Lost Place
### (The Lift closing theme)

We Talk of Dreams

# "Victoria's Lift"

## (Opening Theme)
# Henninger Parke Music

A s the old Martin Mull saying goes, "Writing about music is like dancing about architecture." We won't bore you with "C Minor this" and "Staccato that," but if we are gonna dance, let's sashay our way directly to the guts of the building, right to those sliding doors, and take that elevator wherever we are destined to go.

When we were first communicating with Dan about doing music for "The Lift," he had already produced the pilot. Upon our first listen we were immediately struck by the palpable atmosphere that Dan and Cynthia had conjured – it felt like equal parts "Twilight Zone", "Lights Out!" and old EC Horror Comics – and we knew they had something special we wanted to work on.

We were asked to score the first episode and, if memory serves, we wrote the theme unsolicited because we were unable to help ourselves.

Victoria, of course, had to have a music box. The music box represents a sort of innocence that is not naïve but simple, straightforward and wise. It echoes through the bowels of the building and absorbs the darkness of the souls that have walked its corridors.

The Lift itself has a personality as well – it growls. It is righteous vengeance and justice. It is the righting of wrongs in the moral sense and simultaneously it is the terror that each of face if we examine our own shortcomings. Chains move it, cranking it up and down with its cargo screaming in horror at the known destination they are travelling to.

These two elements (without any boring musical terminology – nerds check the sheet music!) – Victoria and The Lift itself make up the whole of the theme we wrote for "The Lift". We have enjoyed writing score for the podcast and always love working with Dan and company and look forward to working with them on more episodes of "The Lift" and other terrifying audio adventures.

Now, if you will excuse us, we have to waltz our way down this dimly lit hallway – we have a button to push.

Kimberly Henninger and Shawn Parke
Henninger-Parke Music

# "Victoria's Theme"

## (Character Theme)
# We Talk of Dreams

For Victoria's Theme, we were creating a melody that would be Victoria's calling card, as it were. It would play when she came onto the scene and would be used as a "reference" throughout the episodic scoring of the show - to give it a cohesiveness.

As with all character themes, this piece was to capture the essence of her character. That being the case, we wanted to create music that was evocative of Victoria's illusive power over her visitors, but also captured her loneliness while still paying homage to the joy and wonder she has when experiencing her world. To do this, we started with a basic melody that Dan had in his head and expanded upon it to create a melody that felt like it belonged to a Victorian music box, but then also added layers so the melody felt like it was swaying, almost trance-like.

As the piece goes on, the more under its spell you become. For the full music box authenticity, I kept the whole piece confined to 2 octaves, and making sure every note had the same dynamic attached to it.

Nico Vettese, We Talk of Dreams

# "The Lost Place"

(Closing Theme)

# We Talk of Dreams

This piece was designed to capture the conclusive darkness, yet somewhat playful, end to the show.

I envisioned Victoria playing with her music box at the end of her tales, after parting from her visitors. There's a looseness to the piece to match Victoria improvising as she makes her way back on her lift, attempting to create a song for her day's outing.

Nico Vettese, We Talk of Dreams

# Drawings from
# The Journal of
# W. E. Bigglesworth-Hayes
(Victoria's Father)

# by Daniel Foytik and
# Jeanette Andromeda

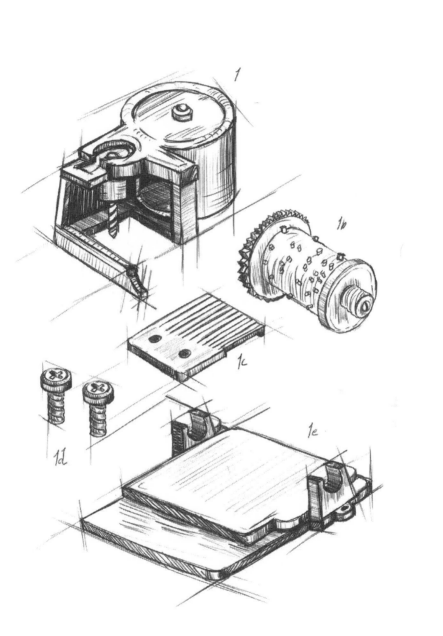

1

1b

1c

1d

1e

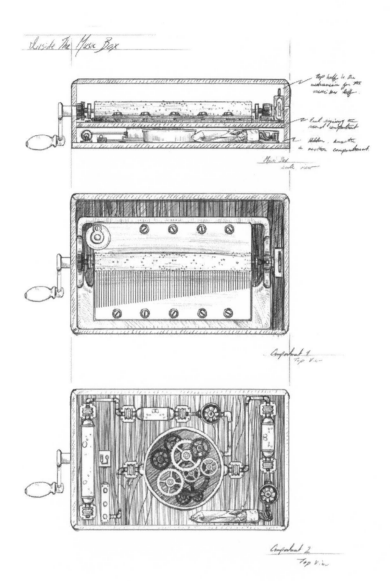

Inside The Music Box

Top half is the mechanism for the music box half.

the tued spring the read compartment.

hidden beneath a wooden compartment.

Music Box
scale view

Component 1
Top View

Component 2
Top View

The Hobble

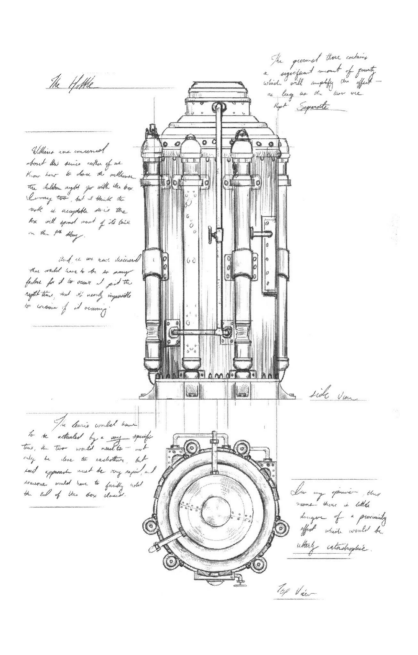

The ground there contains
a significant amount of gravity
which will amplify the effect —
as long as the two are
kept Superclose

Villains are concerned
about this series rather of we
know how to leave the millennia
the hidden right for with the box
leaving too, but I think the
risk is acceptable since the
box will spend most of its time
on the 9th thing.

And as we have discussed
this would have to be so many
failure for I to occur I put the
right time, that it's nearly impossible
to conceive of it occuring.

The device would have
to be activated by a very specific
time, the two would need to not
only be close the eachother, but
said approach must be very rapid, and
someone would have to forcibly hold
the lid of the box closed.

side View

In my opinion this
seems there is little
danger of a proximity
effect which would be
utterly catastrophic.

Top View

# The Collected Notes of Alice Margaret Bigglesworth-Hayes

(Victoria's Mother)

## by Cynthia Lowman

Illustrations by Jeanette Andromeda

6th March, 1936

To Whom It May Concern,

I came upon this box of scraps of poems,
letters, and other writings while sorting through
my own mother's belongings. It appears these
are from another patient of the sanitorium.
Since that facility is now closed, I thought to
dispose of the box until I happened upon this
address.

In the hopes that a relation of this Alice
Margaret is interested in these writings, please
accept them with my apologies for my mother's
apparent theft. If the family is not interested
or unreachable, please dispose of this parcel as
you see fit.

Sincerely,
Evan Young

# Lunar Scythe

In the cooling evening,

I walk

under a fairy tale moon.

A golden crescent,

sharp enough

to prick a finger.

Should I try

to catch it

and slice

the darkening sky,

to escape

...into oblivion.

Erase me.

I am wrong.

Undo
the error.

No fix

remains.

Something has happened.

Something horrible has happened.

They tell me nothing, but I know.

I know.

It is back.

Why does the dark come for me now?

Please, tell me where my children are.

Where are they?

Where did you take them?

The dark lies. But it also tells truths.

It will not take me.

Do not give in. It will not take me.

It will not take me. Do not give in.

Do not give in.

They lie to you. Don't believe them.

Listen.

In the blackest quiet, the answers come.

they are gone! Where are they?

They are gone! Where are they

They are gone! Where are they

Where are they • Where are they

William is gone. • Victoria is gone.

Merritt is gone. • Merritt is gone.

Merritt is gone! • Where are they

• Where are they •• Where are they? ••

William is gone. Victoria is gone.

Merritt is gone Where are they?

Winter Tree

A silhouette of claws
grasping sky
in a death
embrace.
Frozen limbs
in a last
succulent taste
of sunlight.
Failed metawave

# Winter Tree

A silhouette of claws

grasping sky

in a death

embrace.

Frozen limbs

in a last

succulent taste

of sunlight.

Failed sustenance.

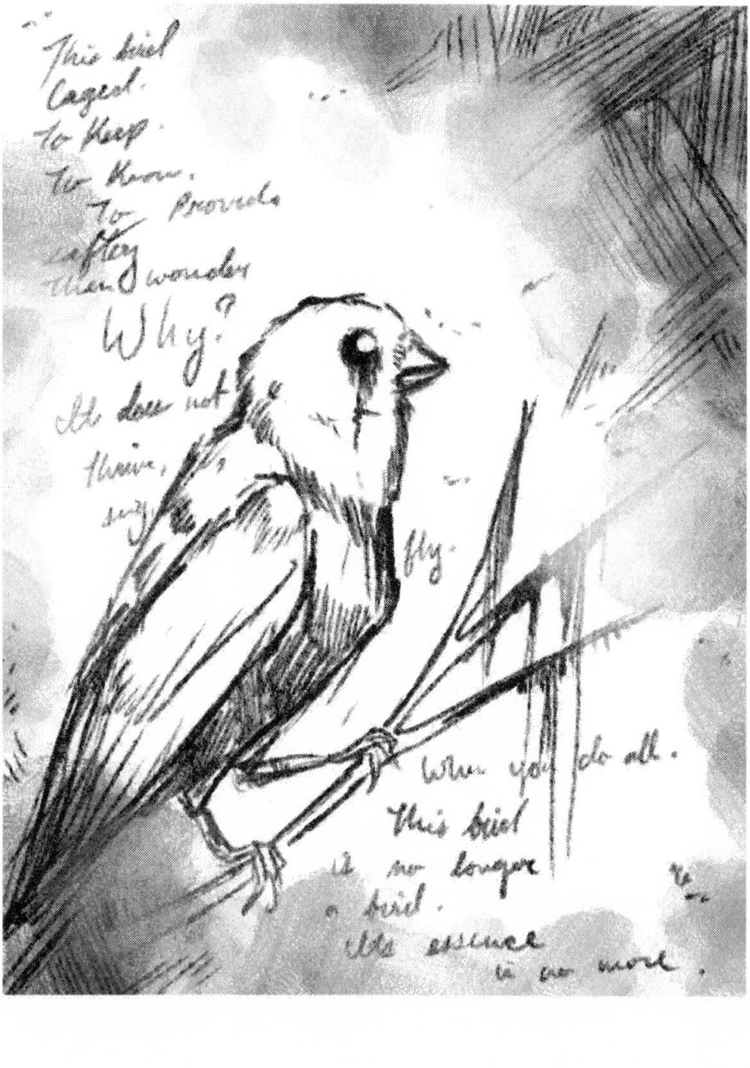

This bird,

caged.

To keep.

To know.

To provide

safety.

Then wonder

Why?

It does not

thrive,

sing,

*Fly.*

When you do all

this bird

is no longer

a bird.

Its essence

is no more.

Terror wind

snaps limbs

bites skin

mangles lives

batters comfort

and dies.

I am unsure of the days I have been here, but it is many. I still cannot keep the number in my head when it is given, for the total is so great as to cause my conscious mind to dispose of it immediately. When I am better still, I may be able to carry the number so far as this page. I am simply pleased to have a page and pen. It has taken so long to get even this.

My time is short though, and I must write what letters I can, rather than indulge with laying thoughts down in ink.

It seems even if I were to write down my days of imprisonment, I would be unable to refer back to it, for my pages were all taken from me and not returned! Why do I bother? It seems my personal writings are, in actuality, correspondence with the staff of this institution. How am I ever to return to sanity if I am not even allowed to do the simplest of my former routines? Perhaps I will no longer write anything at all!

I am but a puppet, strings first held by my family, stolen away by my husband, and finally wrested from him by the darkness that took my children. I still dance, as it seems all of us do. My only freedom is lifelessness. ..•

Promises brought me here, hope of freedom, some semblance of control. William believed what he told me, so does that make it all lies? He did not see how he controlled everything, keeping me bound as I always had been... always will be. I do not question his belief, but that belief shone so brightly that he did not see there was no place for me. I was relegated to wife, vessel, mother, serving encouragement while he did important work.

That work doomed us, put me here, took what minor roles I did have. I am nothing, locked away, forgotten.

I am not myself. He took that from me. Forced me to be who he wanted instead of seeing who I am. I call for him no longer.

He was blind. Perhaps he still is.

Perhaps he always will be. But I see. And I

no longer follow. In some way, I will be myself.

And disappear in his blindness.

The dark is a comfort now.

Dear Doctor Pierce,

When will I be allowed privacy in my own writings? My
personal thoughts being read by you and whomever else,
shall drive me further from sanity, not bring me to it.

I request a personal diary to keep with me. It will aid
in my recovery to have such an avenue of release.

With sincerest hope,

Alice

At last, I have gained some modicum of trust!

While I am still not allowed a pen and ink in my room,
I am able to keep these pages. It is not the small
diary for which I had hoped, but it will do. I take
such joy in small victories, which aids my progress. Or
so I am told.

One trouble on which I must ponder, is my future should
I be discharged. William does not respond to my
letters, nor have I seen him since before I received the
dreadful news of the loss of my children.

I'm afraid I was quite intolerable at times. My anger
for being locked away again was all directed to
William. Perhaps he was finally pushed beyond reach.
Without his accompaniment, I will not be allowed
discharge, for I must have a caretaker.

That leaves me with only one option. My family. I have
not had even a word with them since we moved to

America, and few before that, ever since my engagement to William. But if William is gone, my only choice is inquiring if they will take me in.

Do I have the will to bear their smugness over how right they were that William would bring me to ruin? I am unsure if I can bear their archaic ways. I am also unsure if I can bear being locked away forever.

Date?
William,

I write to you this time as a simple courtesy—one last grace, should you receive it. I do not know if any of my letters reach you, for they are taken, and no word is given as to their path from my room. I presume by your lack of correspondence, whether in return or simply initiated by you, that you have chosen to leave me. I cannot say I am shocked, though I would have expected it of a lesser man than yourself.

You sent me here "to recover and to keep me safe." You think me too far gone to see such a falsehood. But I know.

You are clouded by need and insecurity that drives you away. Through the horrors I, myself, have had to bear, I am able to accept what you cannot. You abandon me to find a reversal for what happened to our children. You will be forever searching. I cannot blame you, for the truth is a horror that I too long denied.

I wait for you no longer. I am much improved, following instructions as I am given. If only you could see me! But this time, I shall save myself.

As much as it pains me, I will go to my family. They have kindly extended an offer to return to their protection. I will likely never see you again, should you have a change of heart. It is too late for us, but I wish you well, as I have always done.

Yours no longer,
Alice Margaret

# About our Authors and Illustrator

**Scarlett R. Algee**'s fiction has been published by *Body Parts Magazine*, *Bards and Sages Quarterly*, and *The Wicked Library*, among other places. She is a regular contributor to the horror flash-fiction site *Pen of the Damned*, as well as to *The Lift*; her short story "Dark Music," written for *The Lift*, was a 2016 Parsec Awards finalist. As an editor, her work includes the bestselling *Explorations* anthologies; the *Survivors* series by Nathan Hystad, and the *Lucky's Marines* series by Joshua James. She lives in rural Tennessee with a beagle, skulks on Twitter at @scarlettralgee, and blogs occasionally at scarlettralgee.wordpress.com.

**Jeanette Andromeda** is a little obsessive. But in a good way. She's an illustrator, YouTuber, blogger and self-proclaimed work-a-holic. Her illustrations have adorned the covers of the novels, *Demons, Dolls and Milkshakes* and *Spiders in the Daffodils* – both by Nelson W. Pyles, as well as in the pages of *The Siren's Call* magazine. Her artwork has been seen in association with the podcasts: *The Lift*, *The Wicked Library*, *Throwdown Thursday*, and *Trick or Treat Radio*. Each week she creates an original piece of horror-themed artwork for her blog, horrormade.com, and promotes the creation of horror haiku with her community on Twitter under #HorrorHaikuesday. She is constantly creating and sharing her artistic adventures on youtube.com/jeanetteandromeda. For everything Jeanette creates check out jeanettecreations.com.

**Lee A. Forman** is a fiction writer and editor from the Hudson Valley, NY. His fascination with the macabre began in childhood, watching old movies and reading everything he could get his hands on. He's a third-generation horror fanatic, starting with his grandfather, who was a fan of the classic Hollywood Monsters. His work has been published in numerous magazines, anthologies, websites, and podcasts including *The Lift* and *The Wicked Library*. His debut novella, *Zero Perspective*, is available from Amazon and other retailers, as well as a collection of short fiction, *Fragments of a Damned Mind*. Find more info on his website at www.leeformanauthor.com.

**Daniel Foytik** is a teller of interesting lies who explores his love of story in all its forms through writing, narration, and the creation of multiple award-nominated and award-winning audio drama podcasts including, *The Lift*, *The Wicked Library*, and *The Private Collector*. His short story "A Little Light Gets In" appears in *Shadows at the Door, An Anthology*, which he also narrated along with Cynthia Lowman. He is the co-creator of *The Lift* but considers himself to be as much Victoria's creation as she is his. Daniel lives in Pittsburgh, Pennsylvania, for now, but has a strong desire to move to the mountains of North Carolina and disappear onto a farm surrounded by deep, dark woods.

**K. B. Goddard** is the author of *A Spirited Evening and Other Stories*. She lives in Derbyshire, England, where at a young age she developed a love of old ghost stories, mythology, and folklore. In 2016 she was delighted to have one of her Victorian-inspired ghost stories published as part of *Shadows at the Door, An Anthology*. Her stories have also appeared on podcasts for both *The Wicked Library* and *The Lift*. In 2017, the Wicked Library episode featuring her story "Shadows" was a Parsec Award winner, and the story she wrote for season two of *The Lift*, "The Lost Library," was a finalist in the same category.

**Jon Grilz** is the creator of the podcasts *Small Town Horror* and *Creepy*, and the *Crazytown* novel series. He has also written stories for both *The Wicked Library* and *The Lift* audio drama podcasts. When not working on what the future holds for the town of Crayton, Minnesota, he can often be found with a confused look on his face, nodding solemnly to himself. He's that sound you hear, the footsteps in the woods when no one else is around. The groan of a floorboard in an empty house. The stifled sounds of weeping any time a student loan bill is opened…

**Cynthia Lowman** is a writer, narrator, and audiobook editor in South Carolina, where she lives with her husband and rescued pets. Cindy is the co-creator of *The Lift*, and has written and narrated short stories featured on *The Lift* and *The Wicked Library* podcasts. She also narrated several stories for *Shadows at the Door, An Anthology*. She has one completed novel too horrible for print and a second one that probably has the same fate. You can intermittently follow her journey on her blog and social media, which she's been told to use and sometimes does.

**Nelson W Pyles** is a writer and voice actor living in Pittsburgh, PA. His latest novel, *Spiders in the Daffodils*, is available from Burning Bulb Publishing. His first novel, *Demons Dolls and Milkshakes*, will be re-released in January 2019, as well as the sequel later that year. He is also the creator and an executive producer for *The Wicked Library* (as well as the voice of "The Librarian.") He has written and performed on *The Wicked Library*, *The Lift*, and *The Private Collector* podcasts. You can find him online at www.facebook.com/nelson.pyles and @nelsonwpyles on Twitter.

**Meg Hafdahl** is a horror and suspense author and the creator of numerous stories and books. Her work has appeared in anthologies such as *Eve's Requiem: Tales of Women, Mystery and Horror* (Spider Road Press) and has been produced for audio by *The Wicked Library* and *The Lift*. She is also the author of two popular short story collections, including *Twisted Reveries: Thirteen Tales of the Macabre* (Inklings). Her debut horror novel, *Her Dark Inheritance* (Inklings), debuted in 2018, and its sequel, *Daughters of Darkness,* is slated for a 2019 release. Meg is also the co-host of the podcast *Horror Rewind.* www.meghafdahl.com

**Charles Rakiecz** is the original "Analog Man," a self-described semi-technophobe who pines for the pre-social media days of yore. He is a retired model builder for the museum exhibit and industrial display industry. Chuck lives in Pittsburgh, PA with his wife, Sue, and their feisty tabby cat, Misty. In addition to his membership in Pennwriters, Chuck is also a life member of the nationally known Western Pennsylvania Model Railroad Museum. It's no surprise that his very first published piece was an article that appeared in the November 1967 issue of *Model Railroader.* Chuck is the author of three stories featured on *The Lift* podcast, and co-author of one featured on *The Wicked Library.* He acts as Coordinator of the Pittsburgh East Writers critique group and is currently working on a time-travel thriller novel, *Point in Time.*

**Brooke Warra** grew up in a little house in the deep dark wood where she developed a taste for the macabre. Her work can be found in various venues including *Strange Aeons* magazine, *The Wicked Library* podcast, *The Lift* podcast and the Dim Shores anthology *Looming Low.* She lives and writes with her family in the Pacific Northwest. You can learn more about Brooke and her writing at brookewarra.com.

# Thank You

Many people are involved in breathing life into a collection this nature. So many that if I attempt to name more than just a few, I'll leave someone out, which would be horrible. So I will instead name just a few, and mention the rest as part the groups they belong to. Know that if you've be a part of this experience, I am deeply thankful to you.

When I started The Lift with my friend Cynthia Lowman, it was always my hope that there would one day be a written collection of stories like this, set in the world of The Lift. It's been an amazingly fun and incredible ride to get this point, but I couldn't have done it alone.

I'll start by thanking my mother, Linda, for encouraging my love of story and writing, because without that foundation this never would have happened. A big thank you my wife, Monica, for letting me use so much solitary time to peruse my creative projects and encouraging me to continue when I needed it. A huge thank you to my friends Cindy and Chuck, for actively discussing my ideas for an audio drama featuring Victoria that eventually became The Lift. I need to thank Scarlett Algee for her tireless work editing, her encouragement, conversations and her unwavering enthusiasm for the project. And, similarly, I need to thank Aaron Vlek for editing Scarlett's story. I need to thank Jeanette Andromeda for her amazing work on the illustrations, and Jeanette and her husband, Alexander, for their work on the book trailer. Nico Vettese and his work on the score for the same trailer also deserves my deepest thanks. Thank you also to Greg Shaffer, my designer for logo design and color study.

Of course, I need to thank the writers, the composers, the artists, the voice actors, and everyone else who has been a part of bringing this world to life. All of you have been a huge part of this project. It would not exist without you. And, I'd be remiss to not thank my fellow podcasters and audio drama creators – such a great community who have been there to commiserate with in those times when I needed it most. The only people who understand what it takes to make a show like The Lift, and how to pick you up when the sheer amount of work brings you down, are other audio drama creators.

I've had the great privilege to work with so many talented artists who have become people I respect, admire and many who are now dear friends. Working with all of you on The Lift has transformed me forever and made me a much better version of myself; I'm thankful to all of you for this.

Thank you to Victoria, my begotten, spiritual daughter and Guide. She has been extremely patient with me, but she also constantly forces me (kicking and screaming at times) to become a better storyteller. She will always be the embodiment of the best part of me, and I'm grateful to her for what I know will be a lifelong ride.

And, of course, I must thank you, the listeners and (now) readers who have allowed Victoria to become a part of your lives. Thank you to those who have donated to the show, bought this book, and written amazingly candid and touching reviews sharing how the stories have transformed you in ways I could have never imagined. Your love of Victoria and her world is humbling beyond words.

Daniel Foytik
October 2018

Made in the USA
Columbia, SC
17 January 2019